Also by Ron Schwab

Sioux Sunrise
Paint the Hills Red
Ghosts Around the Campfire

The Lockes
Last Will
Medicine Wheel

The Law Wranglers
Deal with the Devil
Mouth of Hell
The Last Hunt
Summer's Child

The Coyote Saga
Night of the Coyote
Return of the Coyote

Summer's Child

The Law Wranglers

Ron Schwab

Poor Coyote Press
OMAHA, NEBRASKA

Poor Coyote Press
P.O. Box 6105
Omaha, NE 68106
www.poorcoyotepress.com

Publisher's Note: This is a work of fiction. Names, characters, places, and incidents are a product of the author's imagination. Locales and public names are sometimes used for atmospheric purposes. Any resemblance to actual people, living or dead, or to businesses, companies, events, institutions, or locales is completely coincidental.

Ordering Information:
Quantity sales. Special discounts are available on quantity purchases by corporations, associations, and others. For details, contact the "Special Sales Department" at the address above.

Summer's Child/ Ron Schwab -- 1st ed.

ISBN 978-1943421282

Summer's Child

The Law Wranglers

1

OLIVER WOLF AWAKENED instantly when he heard footsteps in the second-floor hallway of the Exchange Hotel. He had spent his first few months in the city sleeping on the stage of the Teatro Santa Fe where he spread out his bedroll after working hours and was often visited by its director, Jessica Chandler. After receiving payment for the stage expansion work he had completed for the theater and selling one of his paintings, he took over the rooms formerly occupied by his friend, recently married Josh Rivers.

Jessica, who resided in a room at the opposite end of the hall, evidently came with the room, for she and Josh had once been lovers, and now she was nestled naked beside him in the bed. She seemed more familiar with the room than the tenant was.

Wolf swung his long legs over the side of the bed and reached first for his Army Colt and then his trousers. By the time the walker paused at the door, he had his pants on and had stepped into the cramped living area, his gun pointed toward the door. There were a few soft knocks on the door. He flattened his back against the wall adjacent to the doorway. "Who is it?"

"It's me, Oliver. Chance Calder."

"Chance? What in the hell do you want at this hour?"

"Let me in and I'll tell you."

Wolf released the deadbolt and opened the door, taking care to let Calder clear the entryway before he stepped out and closed the door. Marshal Chance Calder, a wiry five and a half feet tall, as usual, was dressed in a sharply-pressed black suit and string tie with a white Stetson pulled low on his forehead. His neatly-trimmed moustache and long sideburns were a distinguished salt and pepper gray.

"You are kind of a careful man, aren't you?" Calder said.

"Habit. Now what's this about? It's not five o'clock yet."

"I'd like to have you make a visit with me. I'll deputize you."

"What's the pay?"

"A steak supper at the Exchange."

"United States Marshal ought to do better than that."

"Budget problems."

Wolf and Calder had become friends when the marshal was a top sergeant with Colonel Ranald Slidell Mackenzie, and the Cherokee, then known as White Wolf, was an army scout. As the Comanche wars wound down, Wolf chose not to renew his contract with the military, and Calder took retirement. Coincidentally, they both ended up in Santa Fe.

"Where are we going to visit this time of day?"

"Judge Robinson's town place. Burned down last night. The stableman, Moses Monroe, said three riders, with flour sacks covering their faces, rode up to the house, tossed torches through the windows and skedaddled. At first, Mose said he thought the Klan was coming . . . he's a former slave. He ran for help, but at that hour couldn't roust anybody but spectators. He finally came to my place, but by that time all we could do was watch it burn and stomp out any sparks that came close to the stable."

"Don't you have a fire brigade in this town?"

"Nope. Fires pretty much have free rein in this part of the country."

"It sounds like it's too late for me to help put out a fire. What do you expect me to do?"

"I'd just like to have another set of eyes go over the place with me. Obviously, there's criminal conduct involved . . . arson at the least. This is a federal territorial judge we're talking about. And Judge Robinson is going to be royally pissed and will expect results from the marshal's office."

"The judge wasn't home?"

"No. Moses thought the judge was in town. I think he knows where, but he insisted it wasn't for him to say. Mrs. Robinson had mentioned in the afternoon that someone from her father's hacienda would be picking her up later in the evening and that she would be spending several nights with her parents. He was stingy as hell with his words, and I will need to follow up with him later."

"Okay. Tell me how to get there. I'll finish getting dressed and meet you at the house."

"Much obliged. The residence . . . or what's left of it . . . is only about three blocks east of the Plaza. Just follow the smoke."

After the marshal departed, Wolf slipped his feet into ankle-high moccasins and then pulled on a flannel shirt patterned with Navajo symbols. The shirt stretched over shoulders and torso sheathed with solid, sinewy muscle.

"Josh?" called Jessica from the bedroom. "What are you doing?"

Wolf stood in the doorway. "My name is Oliver. I have to leave."

"Then you don't have time?"

"I'm afraid not."

"Then I'll go back to my room."

"As you wish. I'll try to stop by the theater later."

"I will expect you. We can put out your exhibit today."

Jessica had agreed to market Wolf's paintings and sculptures in the theater lobby, for a commission, of course. She had given him a nice opportunity, but he had already located a temporary building suitable for a studio-shop. Regardless, he hoped his marketing arrangement with Jessica would outlast their conjugal relationship, which showed no promise whatever of permanence. The slender, raven-haired actress-theater entrepreneur, who was several years older than Wolf's thirty-two, had made it clear she was looking for neither love nor husband. Wolf loved another woman, who seemed unattainable, so their relationship was built on shifting sand.

2

WHEN WOLF ARRIVED at the fire site, he was surprised to find Marshal Calder talking to Tabitha Rivers, the young, yet seasoned, reporter for the *Santa Fe Daily New Mexican*. As he approached, he felt a queasiness in his stomach. Tabby did this to him, and he consciously tried to avoid her these days. It was difficult to do when you loved someone as much as he loved her.

Wolf had first encountered Tabitha when she was a war correspondent during the Red River War. They had become friends before her capture by Quanah Parker's Kwahadi Comanche, and Wolf had made a futile rescue attempt where she refused to escape with him because she had decided to remain and report on the Comanche's last days. During the aborted rescue, he had been severely wounded and would have died if he had not been found by Charles Goodnight, who nursed him to health and christened him "Oliver" after Goodnight's late friend, Oliver Loving.

Months later, Wolf had assisted Tabitha's brother, Josh, whose law firm had been employed by Quanah to negotiate peace terms, in locating Quanah's village. Josh had a dual mission, first, to discuss peace proposals, but, of greater personal priority, to recover his son, Michael, who had been taken captive by the Comanche as an infant. It turned out that Tabitha had been living with the boy and Jael Chernik, herself a one-time captive and known among the Kwahadi as She Who Speaks. Wolf had platonically shared a tipi with Tabitha while they cared for starving Comanche during this time, and he came to realize he would never pluck the young reporter from his heart.

When Wolf was within a few paces, Tabitha turned and greeted him with a welcoming smile. "Wolf," she said, "I never see you anymore. I've missed you."

Wolf shrugged, already feeling unexplainably guilty about his interrupted night with Jessica. "I think you must be too busy these days to have time to miss anyone. I'm surprised to see you here. I thought you had taken a leave of absence from the *New Mexican* to work on your books."

A prolific writer, Tabitha had just completed a romantic novel, titled *The Last Hunt,* which was reportedly enjoying brisk orders east of the Mississippi even prior to its anticipated release four months hence. This was likely due to the fame she had achieved from her reporting during the Red River War. She was now engaged in writing a non-fiction work about the last days of the Comanche wars and her experiences as a female war correspondent. He had heard from Jessica that the anticipated success of the novel had already broken the trail to a lucrative contract for the new book, tentatively titled *Dismal Trail.* No tidbit of gossip got past Jess.

"I still have the prerogative to cover any story I choose. The publisher will pay me on a column-inch basis for any story accepted for publication."

"You haven't had anything turned down, have you?"

She grinned sheepishly. "Not yet."

"Oliver," the marshal interrupted. "I'd like you to do a walk-through with me." He waved Wolf to follow. Without invitation, Tabitha tagged along as they strolled toward the smoldering ruins of the house. The adobe walls still stood, but the roof had collapsed, and the interior had been essentially gutted.

It was like walking into an oven. Red-hot coals still thrived on stub ends of charred and smoking timbers.

The observers had to dodge curtains of choking smoke as they broke a trail through the rubble, and Wolf felt his shirt sticking to his sweat-soaked back. Fortunately for Tabitha, Wolf thought, she was wearing doeskin britches, which had frequently been a component of her daily wardrobe since her return from nearly a year with the Comanche. She evidently found the pants comfortable, but Wolf suspected that Tabitha also enjoyed scandalizing the good ladies of Santa Fe society.

It didn't matter to Wolf what she wore. This morning her chestnut-colored hair, pulled back and tied in a ponytail, glittered in the rising sun. Her flawless, olive skin was lighter than most of the local Mexicans, but she could pass for mixed-blood, even though her brothers tended toward blonde or reddish hair and lighter skin. Tabitha was lithe and willowy and a bit more than a half foot shorter than his own six feet, and, whatever she wore, she was the most stunning woman in Santa Fe.

"Chance, this isn't my idea of a morning stroll. What are we looking for here?" Wolf asked.

"That's why I rousted you out of bed. I don't know what to look for. The fire was set deliberately. Nobody has been able to identify the riders so far, but a crime has been committed. Against a territorial judge, no less. I'd damned well figure this out. I'm grasping for straws."

"Well, I don't think we'll find them in here since the attack came from outside. Of course, any sign out there has been obliterated by curiosity seekers by now."

"I know. But this is so strange. Something draws me to the house. I don't know what it is."

Wolf took the former soldier seriously. Several occasions during Comanche pursuit, he had seen Sergeant Chance Calder's hunches or intuition save a troop of cavalry from slaughter. "What troubles you?"

"If I was going to burn down a judge's house, I wouldn't do it in a way that draws so much attention. I'd sneak up with kerosene or something . . . try to make it look like an accident."

"Maybe somebody was sending the judge a message and wanted him to know it was not an accident," Wolf said.

Calder turned to Tabitha, who was obviously paying close attention to the conversation. "Tabby, if you're going to write this stuff down, beat it. We don't need this stuff in the newspaper."

"Chase," she said. "I'm just getting background. I'll write about what I see. If I'm going to quote you, I'll ask you a question first. Everything else is off the record. I would never do anything to interfere with your investigation. Okay?"

Tabitha was not above charming her way into a story, and Wolf could see the Marshal had already lost the first skirmish.

"All right. But you cause any problems, you'll play hell getting any cooperation from me again. You'll be the last to get the story."

"I understand."

Then Wolf saw it. In the corner of what he guessed were the remains of a bedroom, beneath the debris covering a crushed, tiled tabletop, a woman's bare foot stuck out. He rushed to the spot and began tearing away the rubble. Calder and Tabitha quickly joined him, and in a matter of minutes they lifted away the tabletop and uncovered the naked body beneath it.

"Oh, my God," Tabitha gasped. "It's Constanza."

Wolf knelt beside the corpse, his eyes clinically surveying the woman's flesh, as his fingers gently probed her neck to confirm she was, in fact, dead.

"There are no signs of burns on her skin," Calder said. "Smoke got her, I suppose."

"No," Wolf said, "She was stabbed . . . four or five times, maybe more. Not a butcher knife or a hunting knife. More like a spike or sharp tool. A large awl could inflict wounds like this."

Calder stepped around Wolf and bent over the body, hands resting on his knees. "Fire had nothing to do with it then. She would've been dead before the fire took the house."

"Probably." Wolf looked up at Tabitha. "I don't know the woman. You spoke her name. Who is she?"

"Constanza Hidalgo Robinson. The judge's wife."

Wolf could see that Tabitha was shaken by the discovery. This surprised him somewhat, given the atrocities and carnage she had witnessed during her time as a war correspondent and as a captive among the Comanche.

"I never knew her," Calder said.

Tabitha said, "She was beautiful and fun-loving. About my age . . . twenty-two or three, I think. I suppose she would be at least twenty years younger than her husband. Her father is Miguel Hidalgo. He will be devastated. She is his only child. The family holds an enormous land grant. Their lineage goes back to Mother Spain, and Miguel goes to great pains to make certain others know the Hidalgos are untainted Spanish, not Mexican."

Wolf stood up. "But she did not marry a Spaniard."

"A concession to new realities. Times are changing. Miguel Hidalgo is a shrewd man. He sees that the Anglos will control New Mexico in the years ahead, and his future may well be linked to those who represent our government. A territorial judge was a good place to start. It was an arranged marriage."

Calder said, "It's clear how this young lady died. But that's the only question we've answered. We don't know who killed her. And was it related to the fire? She was supposed to be at the family ranch. So where is His Honor? I need to get a coroner to examine the body, and I don't even know who that is."

"You don't know who the coroner is?" Wolf asked.

"None of the docs want this work for a dollar a corpse . . . greenback, not silver . . . so it's a custom the newest doctor in town gets the job. I'm just not sure who that is."

"Dr. Rand," Tabitha said. "Micah Rand. He opened an office not more than a month ago."

"Very well. I'll contact him and let him know he's the lucky winner. Oliver, would you mind contacting Spiegelbergs' to pick up the body? Alfred Trumble handles the undertaking and furniture sales there. Tell him to hold the body until Doc Rand does whatever he needs to do. I can't guarantee they'll get the funeral work. That will be up to the young lady's family."

"Is there any enterprise the Spiegelberg brothers aren't involved in?" Wolf asked.

"Might be. I just don't know what it is."

The five Spiegelberg brothers operated Spiegelberg Mercantile, a huge general store and had recently established the Second National Bank of Santa Fe. A hardworking Jewish family with a reputation for honesty, the brothers were always alert to a commercial void to fill in the growing community.

The marshal turned to Tabitha. "I know I can't keep you from writing this up. But no quotes from me. Understood?"

"Understood. I'm not ready to do the story yet anyway. I need to know more about this."

"You learn anything, let me know. Maybe we can horse trade a little information."

"Now you're talking my language, Marshal."

"Oliver," the marshal said, "I was serious when I said I was appointing you deputy. Will you take the job? I need some help with this."

"You never did say what the salary was."

"You can put in a claim."

"I'm Cherokee. I happen to know claims filed with the U. S. government aren't worth spit."

"But you'll take the chance. Right?"

"For this case only. And I choose my hours. I have paying work lined up."

"Meet me back here in an hour. I'll bring a badge. We need to sift through the rest of this and hope we don't find any more bodies."

3

WOLF LINGERED NEAR Constanza's body for a time after Marshal Calder left, and Tabitha remained with him. She sensed that Wolf, a stoic, quiet man, was touched by the young woman's death. He began unbuttoning his shirt and stripped it off, before he knelt and gently spread it over Constanza's breasts and thighs.

She scolded herself for her thoughts at this sad moment, but she could not draw her eyes from Oliver Wolf's magnificently-muscled shoulders and chest and abdomen. She had shared a brief chapter of her life with him during the last days of the Comanche wars, and she had lusted for him then, but her self-discipline prevailed—generally to her regret.

The former White Wolf was certainly the most complex man she had ever known. He was in his early thirties, probably ten years older than she, and he had fought for the Confederacy as a major in the First Cherokee Brigade. She knew his half-Scottish father, a career soldier and cavalry colonel, had died fighting the Yankees at Antietam. Oliver had confided he had once been engaged to a young Cherokee woman, but, assuming he had been killed in action, she had married Oliver's twin brother. He understood and forgave, but he did not want to make a life near his twin and former lover and their growing brood of children. He moved on. This man was an enigma to her, more than anyone she had ever encountered. Yes, he had the heart and the courage of a warrior, but he had the soul and sensitivity of a poet and artist. Sometimes, she wondered if the two sides of Oliver Wolf were at war.

"I have Smokey with me. If you like, I can ride down to Spiegelbergs' and ask Alfred to get over here with a wagon as soon as possible. You can go back to your rooms and pick up another shirt, and I'll meet you back here."

Wolf rolled his eyes and surrendered traces of a smile on a face that tended toward the solemn. "I suppose I shouldn't strut around like a naked savage now that I'm a representative of the law, such as it is. Besides, I wouldn't want the deputy's badge pinned on my bare chest."

"Only if you let me do it."

He squinted one eye and looked at her, obviously uncertain how to take her remark. He could take it however he wanted as far as she was concerned. She walked away, heading for the smoke-colored gelding that was hitched in front of a nearby residence.

An hour later, Tabitha and Wolf, with a deputy marshal's star pinned above the pocket of his buckskin shirt, were working their ways through the remaining rubble. Each carried new shovels Tabitha had purchased at Spiegelbergs'. Having been unable to locate Judge Robinson yet, Marshal Calder had embarked on the unpleasant task of informing Constanza's parents of her tragic death. The three-mile ride out to the Hidalgo hacienda would seem like thirty, Tabitha figured. The duty of notifying next of kin would have to be among the most distasteful of a lawman's job.

The undertaker and his young Mexican helper, after wrapping Constanza's body in a blanket, had taken her to the funeral parlor in a rickety cart drawn by a single horse. It seemed like such a humble ending for a young woman of such refinement and elegance. Pop had often said that the Grim Reaper was the great equalizer, and Tabitha had seen enough of it to agree. No man or woman was handsome or beautiful after death struck, or intelligent or rich. The equality of nothingness.

Tabitha turned over charred and smoking timbers with her shovel blade and scraped away burned-out cinders on the tiled floor, occasionally uncovering an item of jewelry or an undamaged vase. Anything that might have value, she placed in clusters, so that family could easily locate them. It occurred to her she had no idea what she was looking for, but she supposed she would recognize it if she stumbled onto it.

She noticed that Wolf was still focused on the room where Constanza's body had been discovered. She decided his location would be the source of any story and changed her course and, trying to appear casual, inched her way in his direction. As she approached him, she asked, "Finding anything of interest?"

"Just thinking. It's strange she was under the table-top. There are blood splatters further out on the floor and on the bedspread. She must not have died instantly and somehow crawled under the table . . . trying to escape her attacker, perhaps."

"Why was she naked? She didn't have as much as her wedding ring on. A thief who raped her?" Tabitha asked.

"I hadn't thought of that. I imagine a woman like this would have had a nice set of wedding rings."

"Oh, yes. The settings probably took a diamond mine to fill."

"I wouldn't think judges make that much money."

"The Honorable Andrew Robinson has been very successful leveraging his government position into a small fortune of his own, along with whatever his wife brought to the marriage. He is rumored to be a member of the Santa Fe League."

"Santa Fe League? What's that?"

"I've been working on a story, but I don't have enough proof to publish. It's a simple scheme involving an unofficial group of businessmen and government officials who have formed an alliance to be first at the government teat. The businessmen buy from, or sell to, government procurement agents, who take a nice illegal commission for their services. For instance, the agent buys cattle at more than top price for the army or Indian agency, and the seller pays him an agreed upon fee. Then, somehow only half the cattle make it to the reservation. Those that don't get rustled by unscrupulous ranchers. For an agreed price, the agent and his drovers look the other way while part of the cattle are being driven off. The same principles apply to almost any commodity. Pop always says government is where the money is."

Wolf nodded, signaling that he understood the process. As usual, his face betrayed nothing.

Wolf said, "You seem to have been acquainted with Mrs. Robinson. Any guesses why somebody might do this to her?"

"We were friendly, but I didn't know her that well. Josh knew her better."

"They were friends?"

"I wouldn't say this to anybody but you. I know you'll be discreet. They were more than friends. They were lovers."

"Your brother seems to have been a busy man."

"As near as I know, Constanza and your good friend, Jessica, were the only two women Josh had an interest in during the five years after his wife, Cassie, was killed by the Comanche. And he was monogamous during his relationship with each of them. I don't know what happened between them, but I think he was very close to marriage with Constanza. I'm sure she loved him . . . enough that rumors had it that she was prepared to defy her father when it came to an arranged marriage. While I know Josh cared for her, he evidently did not share her intensity."

"Her death will be a shock to him then?"

"Oh, God. I hadn't thought about that. I'll have to send him a telegram at Fort Sill. He should at least know what's happened."

"You said Constanza's marriage was arranged by her father and Judge Robinson. Is it possible she had a lover?"

"I suppose. She and the judge had been married less than a year. She had a temper, and the judge is not known for his tolerance in the courtroom. He's said to be a pompous ass, with a cruel, vindictive streak. They might have come to love each other, but they probably had some explosive moments."

"It's possible that the fire and Constanza's death are unrelated," Wolf said.

"I suppose, but it would be an unlikely coincidence, I should think."

"But possible. I'm not a professional detective, but it seems to me I shouldn't eliminate any scenario until overwhelming evidence eliminates it."

"Spoken like a true deputy marshal. I'm impressed with your approach."

"Enough that you would join me for a late breakfast at the Exchange?"

"Yes, I'm starving, and I'm easily persuaded. I'll drop off a story I did yesterday at the *New Mexican*, and then I'll meet you in the Exchange dining room."

Tabitha hurried away to deliver her story, but as she approached the newspaper, she noticed a Navajo woman, with a shawl pulled over her head, standing near the entrance and staring at her. As she drew nearer, Tabitha confirmed that she was not imagining the woman's interest. She was an extraordinarily attractive woman in her early to mid-forties, and her dark eyes were decidedly fixed on Tabitha. Her face was a mask of serenity and calm.

When she was within five or six feet from the woman, Tabitha asked, "May I help you, ma'am?"

The woman nodded, as if approving of something. "You are Summer's child," she said. Then, she turned and hurried away and disappeared into the blinding rays of the low-lying sun.

4

TABITHA SAVED THE strips of bacon for last, aware, but unembarrassed, that she had already devoured more flapjacks than Wolf. So far in her young life she had enjoyed the good fortune to be one of those people who could eat as much as she wanted without adding pounds to her slim figure. She ate the bacon in small bites, savoring the salty flavor that offset the syrup-drenched pancakes.

"This certainly beats horse meat, doesn't it?" she remarked.

"I won't argue that. Of course, you had an entire winter of it. The Rivers brothers and I didn't show up till spring."

Tabitha had endured the previous winter as a captive-reporter with the starving Kwahadi band prior to the trek to the reservation near Fort Sill in Oklahoma Territory. The army's strategy of killing Comanche horses and cutting off hunting routes had worked 4and driven the last Comanche holdouts to surrender.

"We have hardly spoken," Tabitha said. "How are you finding Santa Fe?"

"I loved the summer. We're a few days from October, and the fall looks promising. I'd like to find a house before winter sets in . . . something that has enough room to carve out a studio for my work and perhaps a display area for sales. Unfortunately, I'll need a loan."

"Talk to the Spiegelbergs. The Second National is looking for customers. I'll introduce you to Willi. He's in charge of the banking. Josh and Jael are going to be looking for a property as well. They love the house and office you redesigned and restored for them near Sill, but they plan to spend their winters in Santa Fe . . . probably split their time about equally between the two places. Jael needs the clerking experience in the office here before she attempts the bar exam."

"She's not prepared for the bar exam already?"

"Knowing Jael, she's probably prepared. But according to her last letter, she has to clerk for two years before she can take the bar. But she'll be a cinch. She was more than an interpreter for Quanah. She was for all practical purposes his legal counselor for several years before they went to the reservation. She helped him lay the groundwork for surrender."

"Her language skills should be useful in Santa Fe."

"Her Comanche won't be too useful here, but the Spanish will. She speaks the language without accent, and she found a Mexican soldier at Fort Sill who is tutoring her in the written language. She offered to translate my books to Spanish just for the practice. I think she was only half joking."

"Speaking of your books. Rumor is that you have contracts."

"I do. It's exciting. A New York firm will publish and promote both books. Strangely, they are more excited about financial prospects for the fiction book . . . I'm calling it *The Last Hunt*. It will be set in the last days of the Comanche wars, but it's essentially a love story. The manuscript for the novel is with the publisher and already being promoted, I'm told. Actual publication is three or four months away."

"When will you have the other book finished?"

"I have a Remington typewriter at home now, and I keep it busy whenever I find a few minutes. *Dismal Trail* will be ready for publication about this time next year. It's more work because I must be certain my facts are accurate. The novel comes from my imagination, which I carry with me at all times."

Wolf chuckled. "Yes, I remember you had a fertile imagination."

He rarely smiled, and it made him even more handsome. He should do that more often. She would make his smile a personal challenge.

She continued. "My newspaper series on the Comanche's last days will end in a few weeks, but Danna negotiated with the *New Mexican*, and they get first publication rights only. I personally hold the copyrights and will republish a lot of the stories as a collection in the book. I'll add some others that we considered too descriptive and shocking for newspaper readership. The polygamous intimacies in the Kwahadi tipis might be more than some of the good church ladies can handle."

"You'll probably make a fortune off secret purchases."

"I just want to write and sell books so I can afford to write and sell books. Now, we've talked too much about me. I stopped by the Teatro Santa Fe. I saw your sketches of the horse slaughter at Palo Duro. And your magnificent stallion. They brought tears to my eyes. You are very talented, you know."

Owl, Wolf's stallion, was a large, thickly-muscled animal, ink-black in color except for some white splotches on his rump and irregular white circles around his eyes that looked like broken spectacles. Wolf, as an Army scout, had been allowed to claim the stallion and a filly from the Comanche herds before the soldiers killed some twelve hundred of the horses.

"I can't afford to devote full time to my painting and sculpture yet, but I hope to eventually. Since I did the work on the theater stage, I've had no shortage of building and construction projects. I have a list that will keep me busy for the next six months. I have been contacted by a wealthy gentleman who wants to pay me to just design a new hacienda for him. I have heard of people who make a living designing structures . . . architects, I think they are called . . . but it never occurred to me I might do such a thing."

"Are you going to do it for him?"

"I suppose I will. It might be interesting to do the drawings. If he doesn't like my work, I would not expect him to pay me."

"You're much too generous. But I'll bet he likes it."

"Mr. Wolf?" The voice came from behind Wolf. Tabitha recognized Carlos, the teenaged Mexican boy who had started his own message service business. He had employed a younger boy, and they now stopped at most businesses twice a day to see if there were messages to carry. Many of their missives were directed to the telegraph office, but others were local business orders and communications. The fledgling enterprise was thriving, and Tabitha suspected it was the first of many the novice entrepreneur would operate during his lifetime.

Wolf turned to the boy. "Yes, Carlos. Do you have a message for me?"

"Si. Marshal Calder says you should come to his office *pronto*. Judge Robinson has been found."

"Thank you, Carlos." Wolf fished several coins from his pocket and handed them to the messenger, who had no doubt already collected a fee on the other end.

"Wait a moment, Carlos, please," Tabitha said. "I have a message for you to take to the telegraph office." She plucked a pad and pencil from her pocket book and quickly wrote out a message addressed to her brother, Josh, at Fort Sill. She gave Carlos a silver dollar to pay for the telegram and told him to keep the balance, which should be half of the amount. She knew she was overpaying him, but she admired his gumption.

As Carlos hurried away, Wolf said. "Well, my boss summons, so I guess I'd better be going."

"I would tag along, but I know Marshal Calder won't let me in the door. Tell him I'll be visiting later."

"I will."

"And Oliver?"

"Yes."

She reached across the table and placed her hand on his. "Don't avoid me. We went through too much together. I told you I missed you. I meant that. I don't have many real friends. Danna and Jael. And you."

Wolf hesitated a moment. "I'm honored to be considered your friend. And I don't take friendship lightly."

5

THE UNITED STATES Marshal's office occupied a small corner of the Federal Courthouse at the south end of the Plaza. The quarters were cramped and dingy, and like most lawmen, Marshal Chance Calder was forced to supervise a jail in the rear of his allocated space. A separate facility for prisoner detention had recently been constructed several blocks away from the courthouse. But it went unused because the bureaucracy had disregarded the Marshal's request to fund a staff to operate the structure.

When Wolf walked into the office, he was surprised to find that the marshal was entertaining two guests. The judge was slumped over the front of the desk, leaning on his elbows with his fingers cradling his forehead. The normally fastidious judge's hair looked like it had been struck by a windstorm, and his suit was wrinkled and disheveled.

Seated next to the judge was a striking woman Wolf had met on several occasions. Danna Sinclair's strawberry-blonde hair cascaded over her shoulders, contrasting nicely with a fashionable emerald-green jacket. Wolf knew, if she stood up, Danna would nearly reach his own height, probably exceed it with her high-heeled, button-up shoes. She shared a house with Tabitha and was the second-named partner of the Rivers and Sinclair law firm. The woman, in her mid-twenties, was not known to be a criminal lawyer, and he could not imagine what civil business she had here.

"Pull up a chair, Oliver," Calder said. "I understand you are acquainted with Miss Sinclair. Judge, this is the special deputy I was telling you about."

The bleary-eyed judge lifted his head and nodded at Wolf, who noted that the man, who sported a dark pencil-thin moustache, had evidently not shaved for several days. Wolf retrieved a chair from the corner of the room and set it down near the marshal's side of the desk.

"Wolf, so we all start from the same place, here's the story. Judge Robinson says he only heard about the fire and his wife's death a few hours ago when he was notified by one of his clerks at a room he had taken at the

Exchange last night. Given his prominence, he felt he should obtain legal counsel. He contacted Miss Sinclair and she agreed to come with him to my office, with the understanding that her representation may be temporary. Ordinarily, she limits her practice to commercial and real estate matters, and she would need to consult with her partner, Josh Rivers, before their firm became involved in anything beyond this meeting."

Judge Robinson said, "With all due respect, Marshal, I cannot imagine anything beyond this meeting would be necessary."

Wolf noticed the judge's voice was a bit shaky and that his fingers were trembling. That would not be unusual, he supposed, given he had just learned of his wife's death a few hours earlier.

Calder said, "Judge, I think you can understand that we have to include you on the list of suspects for your wife's murder. You had a room in the hotel, and your wife is killed and your home burned down during your absence. Yes, it's likely a coincidence, and hopefully we can clear this up quickly, if you'll answer a few questions. Also, if you prefer, I can turn this over to the U. S Attorney for the territory for any questioning. He makes the final decisions."

"I'll try to answer your questions. I don't want to talk to Reginald Swayne. He wants my job."

Danna said, "Proceed with your questions, Marshal. But I may advise my client not to answer, if I decide it is not in his interest to do so."

"Fair enough. Judge, when did you last see Constanza?"

"Early yesterday morning. We were discussing plans to leave for a week at our cattle ranch sometime before noon."

"But you didn't go to the ranch?"

"No. She said she was not going. That led to a nasty argument. I loved her dearly, but she had a terrible temper and would frequently end up screaming and throwing things. Yesterday was one of those times. That's why I ended up at the hotel. When she got like this, I learned it was the better part of valor to retreat for a day or two. When I returned, it was always like there had never been any unpleasantness between us."

"You did not return to your home last night?"

"No."

"When did you check in to your hotel room?"

"Mid-afternoon."

"You didn't stay there after you checked in, I assume?"

"No. I went to my office for several hours. My staff can attest to that. I had an early evening dinner at the Exchange and then I went to my room. I was very tired."

"Is there anyone who can verify you were in your room from last night's dinner to the time of the fire?"

The judge looked at Danna and gave a barely perceptible negative shake of his head. Danna responded, "I don't think my client is prepared to answer that question at this moment. We may be willing to discuss this after I have had more time to confer with him."

Wolf interrupted. "Chance, do you mind if I ask a few questions?"

"Help yourself."

"Judge, do you have any personal theories as to why your wife was murdered and your residence set afire? Do you think the incidents are related or the timing just coincidence?"

"I have no idea. My public position, of course, exposes me to some risk from angry litigants or criminal defendants who may blame me for the unhappy results of their experience with the court system. As far as murder is concerned, however, I would think I would be more vulnerable than my wife. And the openness of the men setting the fire baffles me."

"Could someone have been sending you a message?"

"I don't know who the sender would be, or what message."

Wolf thought the judge seemed a bit quick with his response to the last question, but he was convinced the man was starting to close the door on his display of cooperation.

Danna evidently picked up the same signals. "Gentlemen, it appears to me that Judge Robinson has told you what he can for now. I'm certain you can understand this is a very difficult time for him. He will likely have other recollections as he works his way through this tragedy. I assure you that someone in our firm, assuming we continue to represent him, will be in touch with you if we have information pertinent to your investigation."

Wolf had great respect for Danna, but damned if she couldn't use weasel words with the best of her profession. In a nice way, she had just said they were not talking anymore, and they would decide if they had something else to say.

After Robinson and his legal counsel departed, Calder asked, "What do you think?"

"I think he's hiding some things, but I'm not sure they have anything to do with the murder. Whatever else folks might say about the judge, I've never heard anyone suggest he's stupid. Would a man of his intelligence have a quarrel with his wife, check into a hotel room, and then go back to the house later and kill her? Setting himself up as the chief suspect, isn't he? Also, I can see the judge using a gun, but a sharp instrument? He didn't look like he was wearing a change of clothes, and while his suit was mussed up some, I didn't see a spot of blood. Stabbing is pretty messy business. I know that from experience."

"You've almost declared him innocent."

"He's not a very big man. Looks pretty soft to me. Working on a serious paunch. He's not strong enough to take her down if she fights. I didn't see any other marks on her body. Of course, he might have taken her while she slept. I'm not declaring him innocent, but I'd have to see a lot more before I would say he's guilty."

"Doc Rand is doing whatever coroners do as we speak. He said he should have a written report later this afternoon. He warned me, though, he's never done an autopsy before. I guess medical school is all lectures. Those fellas start to learn after they get turned loose on patients. He served as an army surgeon for a spell, so he's cut on a few specimens. He's a likable young man . . . not too full of himself. He's not one of those self-declared docs, at least according to the University of Pennsylvania diploma on his wall. He strikes me as smart enough. Our new coroner will meet us at Spiegelbergs' parlor at five o'clock. You'll be there?"

"Try to be."

6

"WHAT DO YOU think Josh will say about this?" Danna sat behind the desk in her office and was speaking to Marty Locke. The lawyer had been an associate for more than a year, and was handling the lion's share of the firm's trial and criminal cases these days. A fellow University of Virginia graduate, Locke was probably four or five years older than her twenty-six years. He had fought for the Confederacy near the end of the war. His lawyer father had been a infantry colonel who died at Gettysburg.

Martin Locke had arrived in Santa Fe seeking a fresh start after losing his wife and daughter in childbirth. Marty was due for a full partnership, with his name added to the firm's shingle. She would discuss this with Josh when he brought his family to Santa Fe for the winter before the end of October.

Marty Locke replied to Danna's question. "You mean about the judge's request we represent him? I don't see why he would care. We're holding a draft for a thousand dollar retainer, and we don't even know if he will be charged with anything."

"Josh despises the judge. Andrew Robinson was close to abetting the theft of Erin McKenna's estate during her Comanche captivity when we first met. If Josh and his brother, Cal, her future husband, had not ransomed her from Quanah, her uncle might have taken everything. The judge's rulings consistently rushed the proceedings to have Erin declared dead."

"And," Locke said, stretching out his southern drawl, "we suspected the judge was a party to a conspiracy to kill Josh and stop his efforts to negotiate peace and end the Comanche wars, presumably because peace would interfere with the profits of some government officials and business people. But we never proved it. And he has offered a nice retainer to get us started on his case."

Locke brushed back his short-cropped, black hair and smiled mischievously, and she saw his steel-grey eyes laughing at her. Marty sometimes had an annoying sense of humor, and his easy-going, relaxed manner was a sharp contrast to her own seriousness and intensity.

"It's not always about money."

"Says the woman who stalks wealthy clients like a hungry cougar."

"But he insists I be lead counsel in the case . . . if there is one. I am not a criminal lawyer."

"Ah, but you will have the best criminal lawyer in New Mexico Territory sitting right beside you, holding your hand every step of the way."

"And who might that be?"

"I'm deeply wounded by that question." He grinned.

It was difficult to stay angry at a man that handsome. Fortunately, he was pursuing Tara Cahill, a young clerk in the office. But at no more than twenty years, she was a bit young for a man as worldly as Marty, wasn't she? Danna shook off the thought. Intimacy with a firm partner could be destructive. She turned back to the topic they had been discussing. "There is an extenuating circumstance of which you evidently are unaware."

"And what might that be?"

"Josh and the murder victim were once lovers. The break-up on his part was without rancor. I think he remained fond of her."

"What about her part?"

"She had a temper. She wanted to marry him despite her father's objections. She probably remained angry."

"Well, Josh is the senior partner of the firm. I guess we have to grant him a veto on the case."

"I'm going to send him a telegram and see if he and Jael can get to Santa Fe a few weeks early. I do have two questions. Based upon what I've told you, do you think Judge Robinson will be charged with the murder of his wife?"

"If the Marshal doesn't find a killer real fast, I would say charges will be filed as soon as the report hits the U. S. Attorney's desk. Reginald Swayne hates the judge, and it's no secret he covets the judgeship. That answers question number one. What's question number two?"

"Why does the judge insist I be primary lawyer for the defense?"

"His concern is that he will be charged with murder of his wife, a woman. It's reasonable that a jury would wonder why another woman would be the face of the defense if she really thought her client was guilty. I don't want to bruise your ego, but there probably aren't more than a dozen female shysters west of the Mississippi. Supply and demand. The judge is no dummy. And he might just think he's got a helluva lawyer, to boot. Or he's counting on your second chair to come through."

7

A S A COURTESY, Marshal Chance Calder had invited Danna Sinclair to represent Judge Robinson at the autopsy report. She was accompanied by her associate, Martin Locke. Wolf was there on behalf of the marshal, who had been cornered in his office by an angry and distraught Miguel Hidalgo. The victim's father was demanding immediate justice and casting accusations at his son-in-law, the Honorable Andrew Robinson.

Alfred, the undertaker, a thin man with a Van Dyke beard, was half hidden in a shadowy corner, his rumpled, black suit hanging on him like a scarecrow's garments, his lips pressed tight and his eyes expressionless. Dr. Micah Rand stood near the wooden embalming table, which was stained by blood and other substances, the identity of which Wolf preferred not to know. The room was curtained off behind an elegant reception and viewing chamber and appeared to have been a storage area at one time. It was windowless and lighted by a few flickering kerosene lamps. Some hostile chemical in the room made his eyes burn. Wolf thought it could have been a setting described by the late Edgar Allen Poe, and it occurred to him that he should paint his own memory of it. Perhaps he would start tonight.

Constanza Hidalgo Robinson's body was laid out on the tabletop and covered with a sheet of filthy canvas. The young physician's face had been grim before Danna entered the room, but he suddenly seemed to brighten in her presence. Rand was about Danna's height and shared her light complexion, except for a sprinkling of freckles across his nose and brow. He had a head of tousled flame-red hair that needed trimming and wore a white surgical smock that added an aura of expertise. Wolf thought Rand might do well to avert his eyes from the young lawyer, but then he saw Danna's eyes were also fixed on the doctor. It was like their matched pair of blue eyes were engaging in a private conversation.

Wolf decided it was time to convene the meeting. "Doctor Rand, we will try to take up as little of your time as possible. This is Danna Sinclair and her associate,

Martin Locke, who are representing the deceased's husband."

Rand stepped from behind the table and extended his hand first to Danna, who returned a firm, lingering grip. "My pleasure, ma'am," he said. "But I regret the circumstances." He then tendered Locke a brief handshake and nodded his head agreeably, before returning to his station at the table.

Dr. Rand then announced. "My office assistant is typing two copies of my handwritten report, and you may each pick up a signed copy after noon tomorrow. I will tell you what the report contains and will be pleased to answer any questions you might have about my findings. You should understand I was just informed this morning, that by reason of being the newest physician in Santa Fe, I am acting coroner for the entire territory. I have done my best, but I worry I might have missed something of importance. I am not offended if any of you wish to have another doctor examine Mrs. Robinson's body and review my findings."

Wolf said, "I'm sure we'll be fine with your report, Doctor Rand. Just go ahead."

Dr. Rand pulled back the canvas sheet to reveal Constanza's head and shoulders. He clasped the head gently in his hands and turned it toward the spectators to reveal the neck, which had now been stitched. "You cannot see the open wounds now, but the young woman received two shallow puncture wounds in her neck."

Rolling the canvas down Constanza Robinson's torso, he continued. "There were three similar stab wounds in her breasts and chest, but the fatal wound was likely inflicted here in the abdomen, where the weapon drove deeply into her large intestine. Here the assailant was evidently focused on doing great damage, for the victim was virtually skewered. Unfortunately, she would not have died quickly. The perforations were clearly stabs, in contrast to slices."

Wolf asked, "Can you identify the weapon?"

"Not specifically. Something very sharp and narrow."

"An awl, perhaps?"

"Possibly. Or an ice pick. Or any one of a collection of thin-bladed implements. I have treated arrow and spear wounds. This would not be unlike the invasion of a slim arrowhead. There is no way I can determine precisely."

Danna said, "I have a feeling you have not told us everything."

"Well, ma'am, there are several things my examination has turned up that I may be guilty of putting off, but they are not directly related to cause of death. First, given Mrs. Robinson's unclothed state, it should not come as a surprise that she had conjugal relations the night of her death. I found remnants of what was clearly semen in her vagina."

"Are you suggesting she was raped?"

Wolf noticed that the physician was a bit uncomfortable with the subject matter and was obviously struggling for the right words to relate his findings to a woman he had never met before. If he were acquainted with Danna, he would have known one could not shock her sensibilities.

"There is no indication of forcible entry, but that does not preclude the possibility of rape . . . how do I say this . . . in a mature woman of some sexual experience. I did find something in her pubic area, intermingled with her own hair. In contrast to Mrs. Robinson's very black pubic hair, there were two strands of reddish-brown pubic hair, coarser than her own. I removed samples of Mrs. Robinson's hair, and I have examined these under my microscope. The brown specimens were not hers, in my professional opinion, and I have taken care to preserve them. If we assume the pubic hairs were deposited in the process of intercourse, they might be helpful to eliminate some suspects, but there is no science that would allow a precise match with any degree of certainty."

Danna said, "Doctor Rand, I'm impressed with your thoroughness, but I sense you are going to top what you have already revealed to us."

"You are frighteningly insightful, ma'am. There is something else that makes this tragedy all the sadder. You see, Mrs. Robinson was pregnant. About three months along, I would guess. A boy."

8

JOSH RIVERS SAT in his private office located in the portion of the family residence partitioned off for Rivers and Sinclair offices. He shuffled through the leases he had prepared for renting some of the Comanche grazing land to nearby ranchers. Quanah wanted to stock the land with Comanche cattle, but the tribesmen had neither the knowledge nor the funds to acquire the herds to fill the land allocated to the Comanche reservation. There was money, but Josh guessed these were Quanah's personal funds, resulting from gold bullion the former war chief had stashed away, bounty collected from raids and trading during the years prior to the surrender. A fortune of nearly fifty thousand dollars had been set aside and banked in Santa Fe on Quanah's behalf by Josh and Jael.

The shrewd Kwahadi, unlike his fellow tribesmen, had figured out that the white men valued this special metal and concluded it might be useful after the end of their freedom to roam the plains. After capturing Josh, Quanah had prevailed upon him to be his legal counsel in negotiating peace terms and eventually entrusted him with the gold. Their interpreter had been She Who Speaks, the former Jael Chernik, who had been a captive with a gift for languages. Jael had become an important counselor to Quanah. Unbeknownst to Josh at that time, the young Jewish woman had claimed his own captive son, Michael, and was raising him as her own.

Josh heard the door open and, then, footsteps in the reception area. Jael was meeting with Quanah on the reservation, and Rabbit, the teen-aged Comanche girl, who helped with reception and clerical work, was off for the day, so Josh tossed the papers on this desk and got up to check on the visitor. It was a baby-faced army private, exhibiting a shy smile.

"Good morning, Mr. Rivers. I've got two messages for you from Santa Fe," the private said. He thrust two yellowed envelopes in Josh's hand.

"Thank you, Jeremiah."

The soldier wheeled and disappeared out the door, and Josh carried the messages back to his desk. He sat down and opened one of the envelopes and unfolded the enclosure. It read: "Josh. Sorry to inform you that Constanza is dead. Time to come to Santa Fe. Love, Tabby."

He could not believe it. The beautiful, playful, life-loving Constanza gone. His life had revolved around their romantic trysts for a time. She had taught him there could be love after Cassie. He had continued to think of her fondly, even though she had refused to acknowledge his presence after the break-up.

He tore open the other envelope and read: "Josh. About Constanza. Need your authorization. Can you advance trip to Santa Fe? Best to you and Jael. Danna."

Josh stared out the single window of his small office, which mirrored Jael's adjacent work space. Tabby and Danna shared a small house, so Danna no doubt knew Tabby was informing him of Constanza's death. They both thought he needed to get to Santa Fe. Their messages made him more than curious. How had Constanza died? And what in the devil did it have to do with Rivers and Sinclair?

"Deep in thought, Love?"

Josh started at the sound of Jael's voice. She was always doing this to him. She moved like a cat, and she still wore moccasins whenever she had an excuse. Today, riding out to the reservation, she had one. He turned in his chair and lightened at her smile. He loved seeing her in doeskins. It reminded him of the wild creature who had captured his heart.

Jael slipped around the desk and lifted his chin and placed a lingering kiss on his lips. "You didn't answer my question."

"Yeah. Deep in thought." He handed her the telegrams.

She sat on the corner of his desk with her back to him and studied the messages, while he studied the curves of her slender back merging with her perfect butt. "I feel you looking at me," she said.

"You deliberately invited the look."

She stood and turned toward him. "Mysterious messages. Who's Constanza?"

Why didn't he see that coming? "She was a dear friend of mine once."

"Meaning you slept with her . . . using the euphemism."

"She Who Speaks use big white man words."

She tried to appear angry, but the cheek with her single dimple always betrayed her. If the dimple showed, she was more amused than mad. "Okay, we've established you slept with her. I'll add her to the list with Jessica. I hope I have enough paper."

"That's the list. I swear."

She shrugged. "It doesn't matter. I'll make you forget the others as soon as we discuss the telegrams."

"Are you serious?"

"Rylee's at her job at the trading post. Michael stayed at the res to play with friends. He's to be home by supper."

"Can we talk about the telegrams later?"

"No. Tell me about Constanza."

"Her name was Constanza Hildago Robinson. She was married to the Territorial Judge, Andrew Robinson. This took place after our . . . our friendship."

"I should hope so. Only a stupid lawyer would mount a judge's wife."

"You make it sound so crude. Like we're animals or something."

"Comanche talk."

"Anyway, her family comes directly from Spain, and the father always made that clear. They are wealthy land grant people. Robinson is a wealthy man in his own right and a very powerful political figure. I'm admittedly curious about what happened to Constanza, but the messages, taken together, tell me it wasn't smallpox. I need to get to Santa Fe."

"Then let's go."

"All of us? Now?"

"Why not? Tomorrow we finish work on anything that can't wait. Now that the Kwahadi are settled in, we're not rushed so much. Rabbit can send a telegram if there is something urgent, and one of us can come back. The mails are moving faster between here and Santa Fe. Quanah knows how to contact the Santa Fe office. He may come this winter to set up banking arrangements anyway."

"It will take us at least three weeks to get there."

"Not if we don't take a wagon. We'll load a few pack-horses and bring spare riding horses and ride like the wind. We'll celebrate Michael's seventh birthday on the trail. He'd love that. He's still a Comanche kid, you know. We'll be there in ten days, maybe less."

"Sometimes, you make my head spin. But it makes sense. I don't want to go ahead without you. And we were going to leave in less than a month anyway. We can just pack the essentials since we'll be back here in the spring."

"Good. Now we'd better get to work."

"Uh . . . you said something about making me forget."

She smiled, her dimple digging deep.

"That's right. I did, didn't I? I am truly surprised you remembered." She reached out her hand and clasped his. "I'll race you upstairs."

And she made him forget for a time there had ever been another woman in his life.

9

JOSH AND JAEL lay in a hay pile in the stable next to the small house owned by Danna and Tabitha. Their son, Michael, and foster daughter, Rylee O'Brian, at Tabitha's insistence, had rolled out their blankets on the parlor floor, giving the couple some much desired privacy after nine days on the trail. Josh lay wide awake on his back, and Jael slept snuggled up to him, one naked leg tossed over his and an arm wrapped across his bare chest. He wanted to reach for a blanket to pull over them to ward off the night chill, which he had not noticed in the heat of their lovemaking, but he feared he might awaken her.

"It's all right," Jael mumbled. "I know you want your blanket."

He reached down, snatched the corner of the wool blanket and spread it over them. It was a bit scratchy but delivered welcome warmth. He wondered if Jael would always be able to read his mind. She was fluent in five languages, but if silence were a language, she spoke six. They did not require much talk between them to communicate.

"I didn't know you were awake."

"I wasn't, but I am now. You're not going to sleep, and I've had a nap. Tomorrow's a busy day. What's on your agenda?"

"Well, I'll spend some time at the office. I need to get caught up with what's going on, and I promised Danna we would talk more about the firm representing Judge Robinson if he faces criminal charges because of Constanza's death."

"Have you decided what you're going to tell her?"

"I don't think I can object. I've told you that lawyers are hired guns in a sense. The judge would be a paying client, and it's not my place to determine his guilt or innocence. Our job is to give him the best possible defense. I personally do not like the judge, and if he had anything to do with Constanza's death, I hope he hangs. I want nothing to do with the case regardless."

"What about me?"

"What do you mean?"

"In a few days, I will start clerking and continue reading the law in the office. It sounds like a fascinating case, and my Spanish skills might be useful with potential Mexican witnesses."

"I hadn't thought about that. You'll be working for the firm. If Danna or Marty have something they want you to help with, it's not my concern."

She planted a kiss on his ear. "You aren't such a bad guy to work for."

"Treat this boss right and you'll get along fine at Rivers and Sinclair."

"That's settled," Jael said. "Tabby and I were catching up, and I barely got to speak with Danna. What about Michael's adoption?"

"I was saving this. I was going to surprise you tomorrow. Judge Robinson signed the adoption decree the day before Constanza was killed. You have been his legal mother for over a week now. I thought I would order a special cake baked, and we'd celebrate at the Exchange tomorrow evening."

She rolled on top of him and started smothering him with kisses. "This is so exciting. It's the second-best thing that ever happened in my life. Just think. Six months ago, I thought I would lose him. I love you, Joshua Rivers."

"I love you, Jael Rivers. But you're crushing me."

She slipped off but still clung to him. "You weren't complaining earlier."

"That was different. What was the first-best thing that ever happened in your life?"

"I'll tell you another time."

"You can be a mean woman."

"Comanche educated."

"Do you think Rylee will have regrets about not letting us adopt her?"

"No. We're family whatever name she goes by. She knows that. She's fourteen years old now and wants to honor her family name. Remember, it's only been a little over six months since the Comancheros killed her parents. I'm going to take her to meet Willi Spiegelberg at the Second National tomorrow and see if they might find a place for her in the bank or mercantile. We can have a conversation in German. He loved it the first time we met, and it was good for me to use the language. In Santa Fe, I hope to find some German and Spanish books. Hebrew and Yiddish might be more difficult. Willi might be helpful."

"I don't know what schooling opportunities they have here. She is advanced beyond anything the schools at Sill can offer. You said her father was a school teacher before he tried ranching, and she's exceptionally intelligent. She has a head for money. There's no doubt about that."

"I owe her my own little nest egg."

"Her, and Tabby's Henry rifle," Josh said, referring to Jael's ambushing of Comancheros with a rifle borrowed from his sister. After her rescue, Rylee had taken charge of marketing her captors' horses, wagon, and looted trade goods.

"If she gets placed right, I doubt if she will need more formal education. If Willi takes her on, she might be buying out his bank in ten years."

"You're right, of course," Josh said. "A diploma is no substitute for hard work and brains. Pop always says some folks are educated beyond their intelligence. The longer I live, the more I see that. You will be one of the best lawyers in the Southwest. And you won't have a college diploma on your wall."

"We do need to see about enrolling Michael in a school. I'll talk to Tabby about that in the morning. She's going to take Rylee and me shopping for some suitable clothing. I probably shouldn't wear doeskins and moccasins in the Santa Fe office. It is different at Sill where the clients are mostly Comanche and Kiowa."

"I can take Michael to the office with me in the morning. He won't like it, but I'll find something to keep him busy. I'm going to try to track Oliver Wolf down, too. We probably don't want to live here with the horses indefinitely. He might have some ideas for finding a place to live. We'll probably require his building skills on anything we can afford."

"Speaking of Oliver, Tabby was certainly talking about him tonight. It sounds like they might have renewed their acquaintance."

"None of your Jewish matchmaking now. Oliver's looking for stability in his life. I love my sister dearly, but he won't find peace and calm with her."

"Peace and calm are no fun."

10

DANNA SAT IN the cramped Rivers and Sinclair conference room, reviewing a list of law volumes with Jael that she should study in preparation for eventually taking the bar examination. Josh and Danna had agreed that Danna should assume responsibility for Jael's tutelage while the Rivers family resided in Santa Fe. Danna was the firm's resident legal scholar, and Josh had not countered her argument that she would be the more patient teacher. Danna had also noted the newlyweds seemed to be a distraction to each other, and she thought a bit of separation might be healthy. She admitted, though, that she envied the couple's comfortable and uninhibited connection. She had no doubt their marriage would happily endure.

Marty Locke sauntered through the open doorway, pulled out a chair and sat down, slouching his lanky frame in the captain's chair. "Hope I'm not interrupting something important," he drawled.

Danna had concluded Marty was a selective drawler. He generally spoke with a hint of a southern twang, but when he had something important to say, the regional accent became exaggerated. She gathered he had something of significance to say. "You are interrupting something important," Danna said, "but I trust you have something of significance to report."

"We won't have to refund Judge Robinson's retainer."

"Go on."

"He's been arrested. Reginald Swayne has filed a complaint charging murder in the first degree."

"Are you serious?"

"Yep. Wolf stopped me in front of the courthouse and told me. Said we'd probably want to know."

"I wasn't expecting this. At least not yet."

"There's a witness. Not to any murder. But a Mexican servant girl claims she saw the judge return to the house before the fire. She says he came out of Mrs. Robinson's bedroom several hours before the riders with the torches came and set the fire."

"We need to find and talk to this girl. Do you know if she speaks English?"

"Wolf said she doesn't speak much English. They had to find an interpreter, but Wolf said the interpreter didn't speak Spanish much better than the girl spoke English, so they had a struggle figuring out what happened."

"Marty, do you want to go to the jail and talk to Robinson? He'll be screaming to get out on bond. In a capital case, I don't know if we can get him bonded out, or it might be so high he can't come up with it. That raises another question. Who sets bond? He's the only judge in Santa Fe."

"Wolf says the judge's predecessor still lives in Santa Fe. Wilbert Marks. Technically, he's an inactive judge. He's agreed to take the case if approval comes from Washington, but that might take up to a week."

"Meanwhile, Robinson stews in jail."

"Might not hurt him to taste the defendant's side. He's a prosecutor's judge, you know."

"Well, for now, I guess you can let him know we're here to hold his hand."

"I can do that. Meanwhile, somebody needs to talk to the servant girl. Knowing the U. S. Attorney, it won't take long for him to convince her to shut up."

Jael interrupted. "Do you want me to have a chat with the young woman? I speak Spanish."

"Excellent idea. Why don't you find Oliver and get the young woman's name from him? Perhaps he will know where to locate her. I think the marshal's office will cooperate until the prosecutor clamps down. Calder's a fair man, and he's only after the truth."

"Oliver Wolf is a friend," Jael said. "I will be seeing him in a few hours. Josh and I are meeting with him to talk about finding a place to live. He has an idea he wants to share with us."

"Then Wolf and the servant girl are your jobs. Marty, it's up to you to placate Judge Robinson. While you're speaking with him, would you mind asking him for a pinch of his pubic hair?"

"You're serious, aren't you?"

11

WOLF LED THE way, mounted on his big stallion, Owl. Josh and Jael followed on their horses, as they climbed into some low bluffs several miles northwest of Santa Fe. At the top, they came out upon a mesa carpeted with thick, dry grass, surrounding an obviously abandoned adobe house and several outbuildings, including a large barn.

The exterior house walls were pocked and crumbling in places, but the structure appeared stable, and the tile roof looked to be in excellent condition. They dismounted and hitched their horses to a rotting rail in front of the house. Then they pushed open the heavy, sagging door and entered a spacious, austere room, which evidently served the occupants as a parlor or sitting room.

"The door is fine," Wolf said. "It is hinged with leather straps that are rotting away. The blacksmith is manufacturing some quality iron hinges and deadbolt locks that will solve any door problems."

They strolled about the house. It was small, but it had three bedrooms and a respectable kitchen with adequate space for seating their small family. A nice-sized, walk-in pantry off the kitchen seemed to catch Jael's eye, Wolf noticed.

"It doesn't have nearly the space of your Fort Sill residence," Wolf said. "But you will not require office space here."

Jael said, "Oliver, remember, I lived in a tipi for almost eight years. Most houses are like palaces to me. And I'd be fine living in a tipi again so long as Josh and the kids were with me. Well, perhaps Josh and I could have our own tipi."

Josh blushed slightly. "Could we hire you to help us fix up the place if we bought it?"

"Yes, I would supervise and plan it. I have several Mexican craftsmen working on some other jobs I am handling. I hope to keep them working full-time so I don't lose them."

"Who owns the property? How much land goes with it? And, of course, how much money are they asking? We would need to see about a loan."

"I was coming to that. The buildings are set on nearly one thousand acres of grassland. Not near enough for any serious ranch. The owner doesn't want to get involved in splitting up the place, and he wants five thousand dollars for the entire tract with the buildings."

"That's a hefty price."

Wolf smiled. "Jael might be able to talk him down a little, if she negotiates in German. She can probably get a loan as a part of the deal. The Second National Bank owns the place. They got the property back in foreclosure. Willi Spiegelberg is the man to talk to. But I have a proposal first."

Jael said, "Oliver, you are a devious man. You are a good friend, but I suspect an ulterior motive."

"Guilty. I want you to buy the entire parcel with the improvements and then sell me five hundred acres of the grassland. I want to build my own house and a studio on my half. I'll add a stable, so I can breed and raise a few horses. I'll rent whatever grass you don't need from you. I'll put my house within sight of yours, so I can keep an eye on your place when you're at Fort Sill. You mentioned living in a tipi. I want to set up a lodge or tipi out here while I'm building my house. It may take me a year or more, but I can save a lot of money and be near the building site."

Josh said, "You have this all figured out don't you?"

"All but the money."

"We would be getting the buildings, so we could sell you half the land for a fourth of what we pay. Does that sound fair?"

"Yes, I think that's reasonable. I am doing a project for Lucien Maxwell at the First National Bank. I'll see about a loan there. I'll give him a first mortgage on my part of the land and pay as I build, so his security will get better as I improve the property."

Josh said, "I think we've got a deal. What do you think, Jael? Do you want to talk to Willi?"

"Yes, but you come with me. I am still learning the complexities of the real estate business, and the language of mortgages and financing is still foreign. When the Comanche thought of property, he had horses in mind. Of course, Quanah is starting to master the subject very quickly."

Wolf said, "Let's talk to our bankers and get together again in a few days."

"I have something else to ask you, Oliver," Jael said. "Our law firm is going to represent Judge Robinson. I have been assigned the responsibility of interviewing the house servant who came forth as a witness. Can you tell me her name and where I might find her?"

"I guess the judge's lawyers would be entitled to that information. Or they ought to have it. Her name is Luisa Cortes. She lives in a small house with her mother on the first corner east of what's left of the judge's hacienda. I came across her while I was checking with neighbors about anything they had seen or heard that night. She doesn't speak much English, and my interpreter was not the best. I wish the U. S. Attorney had held off on filing charges until he had a complete interview and a competent translator."

"Do you think she will be willing to speak with me?"

Wolf shrugged. "She might, especially since you can speak Spanish. I'll warn you that Tabby thinks she has a huge story playing out, and she's been trying to wheedle the name of the witness out of me. I told her she would have to get any information from the marshal or Reginald Swayne. Of course, they've clammed up."

12

JAEL WAS CERTAIN the fat man was following her. He was not Mexican. He wore a sombrero, but the portion of his face that was not burnt raw by the desert sun was covered with a scraggly blond beard. He was armed with a pistol holstered low on the hip beneath a pendulous belly. She could not imagine why anyone would want to follow her. She was more curious than concerned. She carried a loaded Navy Colt in her shoulder bag, and Tabitha had taught her how to use it with some proficiency.

As she approached the door of the Cortes house, she discreetly turned her head and caught another glimpse of the fat man. He was smoking a cigarette and doing a poor job of portraying a loiterer along the dusty street near the charred remains of the Robinson compound.

She knocked lightly on the door. She tapped again, more harshly this time, hoping to signal her determination. This time the door cracked open and a pair of dark eyes peered out.

"Senorita Cortes?" Jael, speaking Spanish, introduced herself and explained that she wished to ask a few questions.

The young woman opened the door and invited her in. It appeared that the house consisted of no more than a single bedroom and the parlor, which at one end included a wood stove and small table and some shelves with cooking utensils and a scattering of food supplies. Luisa Cortes gestured for Jael to sit on the settee, which appeared to double as an extra bed. Luisa slipped onto a straight-backed chair nearby.

Jael noted that the little house was immaculate and smelled of cinnamon. Luisa was a petite young woman and quite pretty, Jael thought, likely no more than seventeen years of age. She decided to make no effort to speak English and began posing her questions in Spanish.

"Luisa, I am employed by lawyers who are representing your employer, Judge Robinson. I would like to have you tell me what you recall about the night of the fire and Mrs. Robinson's death. May I ask, what was your work at the house?"

"I was the Senora's personal servant. I washed her clothes, helped with her baths and sometimes her dressing. I made her bed and ran personal errands. Whatever she asked me to do."

Jael could not imagine being assisted with her bath or dressing. She probably would not object to the laundry and bed-making. "Did you enjoy working with Senora Robinson?"

For the first time Luisa smiled and nodded her head enthusiastically. "Oh, yes. She was very kind, and we joked and teased each other. I thought of her as an older sister. I felt very sad about her death. I will miss her so much."

"Were you in the house when the riders came with the torches?"

"No. I left before seven o'clock. The Senora gave me the night off."

"I see. Was that unusual?"

"Oh, no. She would do this, two or three times a week, when her husband was gone. Well, she enjoyed time alone on occasion."

Jael noticed Luisa had become uneasy, probably wishing she could take back some words. "Luisa, think very carefully about your answer to my next question. You will likely be asked this when you are a witness in a court-room. "Did Mrs. Robinson sometimes take a lover?"

"I do not want to defile her memory. She was a good woman. But she had needs."

"So, she did have a lover?"

"Yes."

"More than one?"

"Only one at a time, I believe."

"That's not what I am asking. Did she have several men she would see at different times?"

"Yes. There were two in recent months."

"Who were these men?"

"One, I did not know. She spoke of him, but he was very careful not to be seen. She did not offer his name, but she said he was very attentive and was in love with her. Men adored her and would do anything for her favors, I think."

It appeared that Luisa was a bit envious of her mistress. "And who was the other?"

"You will not tell anyone?"

"I cannot promise. But it will not leave our office unless it is necessary to save Judge Robinson's life."

"The other man was Reginald Swayne. The prosecutor. Senora said he was a stallion. Do you understand?"

"I think I do." My God. What had she stumbled onto? What did this mean?

"Do you think she was planning to see one of those men that night?"

"Possibly. It was not my concern. She would often tell me afterward, but not before she had her tryst. She said she and the judge had quarreled, and he was going to the ranch. But, of course, he did not."

"You saw him here?"

"Just before I left. He entered the house and appeared angry. He did not see me, but I watched from the hallway. He walked directly to her bedroom and hammered loudly on the door. They did not share a bedroom."

"And did she let him in?"

"Yes. She was very calm and loving with her voice and I saw her embrace him. I heard their voices coming from the room. He spoke loudly, but I could not make out the words. A fuss between them was not unusual, and I did not think much of it. She could be a very charming lady and I had no doubt she would resolve the situation until the next time. I went home."

"Were there any other servants or staff in the house?"

"None. We have a cook, but she does not live in. The stableman cares for the horses and maintains the property. He will drive a carriage for the senora or the judge on occasion and has a room in the stable. He is old and cannot hear well . . . but, perhaps, more than he lets on. He is no fool. You may wish to speak with him."

"I shall speak with him. Is he still residing in the stable?"

"I believe so, yes."

"What is his name?"

"Moses Monroe. He is a Negro. A former slave. It is said he escaped and lived with the Comanche for many years, before he came to Santa Fe."

They were interrupted by a gentle knock at the door. Luisa got up. "One moment, please."

She went to the door and cracked it open, just before it crashed against her body, sending her tumbling to the floor. The fat man stepped in and shut the door behind him. He gave a broad smile, revealing a mouth full of rotten teeth. He was younger than he looked from a distance, Jael thought, probably late thirties. She sat, unmoving, like a statue.

The fat man looked down at Luisa, who had a nasty gash above the eye that was bleeding profusely, and she was struggling to upright herself. He spoke in a high-pitched voice that somehow belied his size. "Well, I am going to enjoy this. Get up, bitch. You first." He walked toward Luisa, ignoring Jael for a moment.

"Unbuckle your gun belt, Mister. And drop it on the floor."

The man turned, his eyes widening with shock when he saw Jael holding the Colt in one hand, the other steadying her aim. He reached to draw his gun, but the room echoed with the roar of gunfire, as Jael drove a bullet into his chest and another into his eye before he crumpled to the floor, landing only inches from Luisa.

Jael got up to help Luisa from the floor after returning the Colt to her bag. As she stood, Luisa looked first at Jael and then at the big man lying stone dead on the floor of her parlor.

"I think he was here to kill us," Luisa said.

"I am certain of it," Jael said, responding in Luisa's Spanish. "Now, we must clean your wound."

A bucket of water that had been pumped from the outside well sat near the stove. Luisa found a shallow pan and some clean rags, and Jael washed the young woman's face and about the eye, which was starting to swell badly

"You will require stitches for the eye. Will you be all right here if I leave to report this and find a doctor?"

"Yes. I will go in my mother's bedroom, and I will not look at this man."

"I am sorry this happened."

"I am glad you were here."

"Do you have a pair of scissors I could borrow?"

"Scissors?"

Jael knelt next to the dead fat man and began to un-buckle his belt. "Yes. I am going to take a scalp."

13

DANNA AND MARTY sat in the conference room, with law books and note paper spread out in front of them. Josh and Jael were at the Second National Bank negotiating with Willi Spiegelberg for purchase of the mesa property and a loan to finance it.

"Jael earned her keep yesterday, didn't she?" Marty said.

"She certainly did. She has a brilliant mind and life experiences that are going to yield great benefits to the firm. Her multi-lingual abilities will be worth gold in the Southwest. We just need to allow her time to digest the books and court decisions. I have no doubt she will be prepared to take the bar when she completes her clerkship."

"Why did we spend all that time in school?"

"Oh, I don't think that was a waste. I, for one, needed the discipline forced upon me by the classroom. Also, I doubt there were many firms that would have taken a country girl from Texas under their wings for a clerkship to read the law."

"Well, as a native Virginian, it was generally assumed that any lawyer worth his salt would get his start at the college Thomas Jefferson founded. There was a bit of snobbery involved, I guess, but those lawyers who were admitted to the bar by reading the law were looked down upon a bit . . . especially by law college graduates. In this part of the country, nobody's much interested in your diploma. All folks care about is what you can do for them."

"As it should be."

"Back to the case before us. You're getting more involved than I expected. Your assistance is more than welcome, but you originally gave me the impression you were only going to be the face of the case."

"I'm intrigued by the situation. And, selfishly, this is turning into the most public case the office has ever taken on. I don't want to be a spectator."

"Have you had a report on Luisa Cortes this morning?"

"I stopped by her house before I came to work. She is doing well enough. Micah stitched the eye, and, of course, it's bruised and swollen today. Her mother works as a cook at one of the grand haciendas, but she was able to stay home with Luisa today."

"So, the good doctor is 'Micah' now?" Marty teased.

Caught. "He asked that I call him by his first name."

"Well, what did Micah think of the specimens Jael collected for him from the man she killed?"

"I think he was a little embarrassed at first, and disbelieving that a lady would have gathered such things, let alone coolly shoot the man in the first place. He's learning quickly the West is not a place for the timid."

"Did he learn anything from the hair samples?"

"He plans to make a microscopic examination today and report to me tonight."

"Tonight?"

"I guess I didn't mention it. He is taking me to dinner at the Exchange this evening."

"A strange place to discuss examination results. But I suppose this is not entirely business."

"Just an opportunity to get acquainted. Changing the subject, you did not obtain a sample from Judge Robinson yet, did you?"

"No, I don't see a great urgency. We have plenty of other things to sort out . . . for instance, the fact he obviously lied when he said he had not returned to the house.

I don't think that's the only thing he's lied about or failed to disclose. He is going to be very difficult to defend. Whether he killed his wife or not, he is going to keep us busy uncovering a heavy blanket of lies."

"This is turning into a swamp. Now we have Swayne as one of Constanza's lovers. Do you think that has anything to do with the rush to file charges against the Judge?"

"He certainly didn't wait to jump on a piece of evidence. The Marshal either didn't ask enough questions or didn't disclose all the answers to the prosecutor. Incidentally, Tabby has an appointment to interview Swayne for the *New Mexican* early this afternoon. Of course, I can't disclose to her what we have learned at this point, or she would really hold his feet to the fire."

"I suspect Swayne's hungry for the publicity, but Tabby generally grants no quarter when she's after information."

"No. And she is not convinced that the murder and fire are connected. Several times she has speculated about involvement of the Santa Fe League in the fire. She has apparently learned some information she's not sharing."

"Perhaps she's waiting to make a trade."

"Likely, I would say. She knows that we're bound by confidentiality where our client is concerned, but some of what we have learned is confidential only because it's to our strategic advantage to keep it that way. We may find it mutually advantageous to barter with her at some point."

"Is it difficult sharing a house with these secrets you are each holding back?"

"Not really. We each have our jobs and respect the walls we sometimes must build between us. It is almost an instinctive thing."

14

TABITHA STUDIED THE walls of the U. S. Attorney's office, which were obscenely covered with diplomas, licenses and various certificates of recognition, interspersed with daguerreotypes and photographs of the esteemed prosecutor with prominent politicians and public figures. The prosecutor smiled at her from the other side of his desk, obviously giving her the opportunity to peruse the evidence of his power and influence. She had to remind herself that her job was to report, even though she already found herself hostile to the pompous ass.

She turned to Reginald Swayne, who was a handsome man by most standards, with a full head of thick, black hair and a neatly-trimmed moustache. She had checked the newspaper's morgue and confirmed he was thirty-six years of age and married with a daughter and son, all living in the nation's capital, no doubt awaiting his return on a great white horse. Tabitha decided to soften him up a bit.

"Mr. Swayne, I want to thank you for taking time out of your busy schedule to speak with me today."

"My pleasure, Miss Rivers. You are a writer of some fame. I have read your newspaper stories about the last days of the Comanche and will be among the first to buy the book. I am honored you considered me worthy of an interview. And I had no idea that your keen mind was accompanied by such beauty."

She could not bring herself to thank him without gagging. She spent some time asking questions about his professional and personal history, and then suddenly turned to the topic that interested her. "You have filed first degree murder charges against a federal judge. We both know this story will have nationwide exposure and will be the talk of Santa Fe. I assume this puts a great deal of pressure on you."

He smiled and preened his thick eyebrows before he spoke. "Not at all, dear lady. It's all a part of the job. I like to think I do my best work under such circumstances."

"Is it awkward for you that the defendant is a federal judge before whom you have appeared many times?"

"I don't take pleasure in it. But awkward? No. Under the law none of us have special privilege. It is fundamental to our system of justice that the law applies to the mighty and the weak alike."

"I have spoken with the U. S. Marshal, and Chance Calder says any information about the investigation must be cleared through your office. Can you tell me anything about the evidence you have gathered that points to Judge Robinson committing the crime?"

The smile disappeared from the prosecutor's face. "First, let me assure you that I would not have filed charges in the absence of very, very strong evidence. I do not take the matter lightly, and I would not have proceeded without clear and convincing proof."

"Can you give me an example without going into specifics?"

Swayne sighed, showing a bit of irritation now. "For one thing, we have a witness who clearly places the defendant at the scene of the murder. I cannot say more than that."

She decided to take a wild shot, acting on pure hunch. "I have been pursuing a story about the alleged Santa Fe League and its influence in siphoning government money into certain pockets. I've picked up a rumor that Judge Robinson may have a connection with the League and that it could be involved in Constanza Robinson's death. Would you have any comment to share about that?"

The prosecutor's eyes narrowed, and he pressed his thin lips together tightly before he spoke. "With all due respect, madam, I know nothing about such a rumor. The League itself is just a rumor that seems to float around this town every so often. And I must say it sounds rather absurd." He stood up and moved around the desk to escort Tabitha to the door. "I really have some other matters that require my attention. I am delighted to have had the pleasure of meeting you."

15

AFTER MEETING WITH Reginald Swayne, Tabitha returned to the tiny office she was now afforded at the *Santa Fe Daily New Mexican* and wrote up the story about her interview with the prosecutor. It was boring stuff, she thought, since she had no facts that would permit her to bring the League into the article. She would ask that it be printed without her byline.

It was nearly six o'clock. Josh's family was staying with her and Danna for a few more days, but Josh and Jael had taken Michael and ridden out to meet Oliver at the property they were purchasing. Jael planned to make a list of rudimentary furnishings that would permit residency of the house while repair and refurbishing was taking place. Josh and Oliver were going to establish some natural boundaries for the land split, so a surveyor could be employed to make the locations official and devise proper legal descriptions. Rylee would be home after she left her work at Spiegelbergs', but she tended to work late.

Tabitha decided to go home and see if she could fix something for supper for her and Rylee. She knew Danna was dining with the new doctor at the Exchange. She hoped they had a nice evening. Her friend deserved it, and she rarely dined with a male for other than business reasons. It was not that Danna did not have occasional opportunities, but she generally found excuses to decline. Married to her work, particular about her men. Like me, Tabitha thought.

When she arrived home, there was still ample daylight, but dusk was preparing to settle in. She led Smokey into a stall in the stable and unsaddled the gelding that had come with her from Levi Rivers's Slash R Ranch. She doted on the horse and hauled water from the pump outside to put in the iron trough that serviced two stalls. Then she tossed some loose hay in the feeder rack and grained and brushed the animal.

Satisfied that Smokey was settled in, she left the stable and walked briskly up to the house and opened the front door. Instantly, the scent of tobacco and stale sweat struck her nostrils. Too late. A rough hand grabbed her wrist and dragged her into the house and threw her on the floor. She looked up and saw two men standing above her, both with flour sacks pulled over their faces, holes in the cloth revealing only their menacing eyes. They were booted and wore gun belts and holstered pistols. A short, stocky man carried a Bowie knife in a sheath on his belt and a coiled whip in his left hand. Despite her fear, she found herself studying the men with a journalist's eye.

"Stand up, woman. Now."

Tabitha obeyed, casting her eyes about for something she could use for a weapon. She had dropped her bag when she was yanked into the room so abruptly, and it lay next to the closed door with her Derringer nestled in it. The taller man stood between her and the firearm.

She faced the taller man, who was standing near enough she could smell his rancid breath. He snatched the top of her cotton blouse and ripped the garment half off, nearly launching her to the floor again. Before she regained her balance, he had torn away the remainder of the blouse and the camisole underneath, baring her small breasts. Her attacker paused, and she could feel his eyes studying her naked torso. She turned to race for a butcher's knife in the kitchen, but his hand reached out and snatched her hair and yanked her back, shooting sharp stabs of pain through her neck. Then his fist slammed her cheek like a wooden mallet and left her reeling. He followed up with a blow to her nose, and blood spewed instantly. Her knees buckled and she slumped to the floor.

She was dazed and disoriented for several minutes but recovered her sensibilities some, just prior to the first jolt of the stocky man's boot heel stomping down on her jaw. She was only vaguely aware after that of somebody repeatedly kicking her ribs, sending shockwaves of searing pain through her body with each blow. Finally, someone rolled her over on her stomach, and she sensed what seemed like claws tugging her skirt and pantaloons over her hips. Then came the cracks, like a pistol popping in the distance, and the lashes slashing the flesh of her back and buttocks. She was certain, then, she was going to die this night. It was only a question of when and how. And this was okay with her. The pain would be over.

Tabitha slipped away into blackness. She did not know how long she had been unconscious when she felt the icy water spill over her face. Her eyes opened, but her sight was blurred, as she tried to see through the tunnel formed by her swollen flesh. She was still sprawled on the floor, and they had rolled her over on her back now. She could make out the hazy form of the taller man standing above her, a bucket in one hand. Off to one side stood the stocky man, the coiled, black whip cradled in his fingers.

"Now you listen close, Missy," the taller man said, his voice muffled and almost ghostly with the flour sack covering his face. She did listen, and watched as best she could, looking for something that might identify her attackers if she lived to tell the story.

"I am listening," she replied in a near whisper.

"We have orders to stop short of killing you. You're going to pleasure us a bit when I finish my little talk. But you cooperate, and you'll live."

They had already won this battle. Let them do what they want. She would close her eyes and grit her teeth while they took their turns. She just wanted to live to write her story. "I'll be no trouble," she mumbled.

"Then listen. Not a word is to be said about the League in your damned newspaper. There is no League, as far as you're concerned. Hear me?"

"I hear you."

"Next time, we won't be coming after you. One peep of this. One word about the League. Somebody in your family will die. You hear me?"

"I hear you."

"Now, we're going to finish our business."

The door swung open and another man with a flour sack-covered head stepped in. "Somebody coming. One rider moving slow. But we got just a few minutes to get the hell out."

"Shit. Maybe another time, Missy. Don't forget what I told you."

She closed her eyes, thinking only of the hurting as she faded again into blessed oblivion. The next thing she felt was pressure on her nose, and she awakened to find Rylee O'Brian kneeling beside her and pinching her nostrils with a bloody rag.

"Thank God, you're awake," Rylee said. "I saw three hooded men ride off like the devil was chasing them. And then I ran in the house and saw you laid out in all the blood. I was sure you were dead. But then I saw the blood running like a river out of your nose, and then I saw your chest rise and fall. I thought the first thing I should do is stop the nose bleeding. It was awful, but it seems to have stopped now. Can you talk?"

"Some," Tabitha croaked. "Is your horse still saddled?"

"Yes, my mare is tied outside."

"Find Danna. Tell her what's happened. She's at the Exchange having dinner with the new doctor. Ask her to bring him with her."

"Will you be okay alone?"

"I'll be fine. I'm staying put till we get more help. Now ride, girl."

16

DANNA AND DR. Micah Rand had fortunately procured a corner table in the Exchange dining room. This afforded them a semblance of privacy not generally available in the establishment. Usually, after six o'clock, the dining room was overflowing. Tonight's menu was steak, fried potatoes and apple pie, so they were spared the agony of choosing. Both selected coffee over wine.

"I'm a Texas girl," Danna said. "My tastes are very simple. If there had been ten items on the menu, I would have ordered what we got."

"My roots are in Pennsylvania. I was raised on a small farm near West Chester. My mother was a Pennock, descended from Christopher Pennock, one of the early founders of Quakerism in America. I was raised a Quaker, but I guess I've fallen. I haven't been to a meeting since I entered college, but the faith is still a large part of what I am. I did medical school at the University of Pennsylvania."

"I never met a Quaker, but you don't look any different than anybody else," she teased. "But I know you were in the Army. It seems an unlikely place for a Quaker, from what I know of the religion."

"The war was over by the time I entered school. I'm twenty-nine years old next month. And my Army role was non-combat. After medical school, I obtained an Army commission and served several years as a post surgeon at Fort Robinson in northwestern Nebraska. Then, I was assigned to Fort Union for a year and got a taste of this part of the country. I still don't know why it got under my skin, but after my discharge I returned to Pennsylvania and joined another physician in his practice. When he offered a partnership, I turned it down and decided to head west to Santa Fe. I either need to make a place here or get the bug out of my system."

"We have very different backgrounds," Danna said. "You're just three years older than I am. But I have no family. My parents and baby brother were killed by Comancheros when I was a girl. I was lucky enough to escape. This is not a unique experience out here. Comanche killed Jael Rivers' parents, and she was taken into the band. Her young friend, Rylee O'Brian, also lost her parents to Comancheros."

"I had no idea."

"I've killed a few men who needed killing. No regrets. Does that shock you?"

"Shocked? No. But I cannot deny I'm surprised. Obviously, during my military experience I saw men killed and maimed. I'm very aware of the violence in the world. I can use a firearm, but I've never fired one at a man. I don't know if I could. I hope to avoid such a test of my upbringing."

Their dinners were served, and, while they ate, they chatted easily about their backgrounds and ambitions. Then, she remembered she had business to tend to. "You were going to report on your . . . analysis of potential evidence."

Micah smiled sheepishly. "I must admit I'm not totally comfortable discussing such things with a lady. But, there was no match. That, of course, simply suggests that the man left no tangible evidence of sexual assault on Mrs. Robinson. It does not preclude his involvement in her death."

"It was too much to hope for. Still, if there is no match with the judge, your specimen would be evidence that another man had been with Constanza. A seed of reasonable doubt as far as the judge's guilt is concerned."

Danna had taken two bites of her pie when a near breathless Rylee O'Brian rushed up to table.

"Miss Sinclair. You've got to come to the house. Some men have beat Tabby senseless. She could be dying."

Danna was immediately on her feet, and Micah followed.

Rylee continued. "I saw three men riding away from the house when I got there. They had sacks over their heads. They looked like spooks. When I went inside, Tabby was laid out on the floor in a pool of blood. I thought she was dead. But she wasn't. Not yet, anyway."

Micah said, "I'll run to my office and grab my bag. But I don't know where your house is."

Danna said. "Rylee, you go with Dr. Rand and then take him to the house. You can ride double. My mare is in the Exchange stable. I'll saddle her and be on my way."

Danna felt greatly relieved when she arrived home and saw that Rylee's horse was already hitched outside. She was not prepared for the condition of Tabitha's battered face and body when she stepped inside, however. Her friend was half naked and hardly a place on her flesh had escaped assault. Her face was bloody and bruised, her nose twisted and out of kilter. Angry, crisscrossed lash marks swept over her hips and rib cage, hinting at the wounds that would be found on her backside. She still lay on the floor, propped up on pillows with Micah leaning over her, pressing some liquid into her mouth with a spoon.

Rylee was on her way out of the house with an empty bucket, apparently to pump some water from the well. Darkness had settled on Santa Fe now, but the parlor was well-lighted from three oil lamps Rylee had no doubt scavenged from other rooms.

Danna knelt beside Micah. "Will she—?"

"She will make it. This young lady's too tough to die, but she's going to be hurting for a good spell. I've just given her a healthy dose of laudanum. It will dull the pain while we start patching. We need to move Tabitha to a bedroom."

"She has her own room. She lives here with me."

The young physician inched his hands under Tabitha's still form, oblivious to the blood that started soaking his shirt sleeves. He lifted her into his arms and then, amazingly, Danna thought, brought himself effortlessly to his feet. "Lead the way," he said.

Danna found some old and tattered blankets to spread over the covers, and Micah eased Tabitha onto the bed. Rylee returned with the water bucket.

"I have checked her ribs. Someone kicked her viciously, but I didn't detect any broken ribs. They will be badly bruised and will probably cause her the most acute and long-lasting pain. Her nose is broken and that needs immediate attention. The bleeding will likely start when I set it, so gather what clean rags you can."

Tabitha's eyes opened. "What are you doing?" she murmured.

"Just lay your head back and relax, Tabitha. I'm Dr. Rand. I'm here to help you. Danna and Rylee are with me. You're safe now."

Micah gently placed a hand on each side of her nose, probing tentatively with slender fingers. Suddenly there was a pop, like a broken tree branch cracking, followed by Tabitha's scream. "You son of a bitch. What did you do to me?"

Micah smiled benignly, his eyes focused on the nose as if admiring his craftsmanship. As he predicted it began to bleed again, but he pushed Tabitha's head back and pressed a rag compress to her nostrils, and the bleeding quickly abated. He plucked a small scissors from his bag and cut some small strips of cloth from a rag and packed the nostrils. Tabitha had dropped off into her stupor again and did not protest.

"If she follows my instructions, her nose will be fine. She may be left with a tiny bump on the bridge but nothing that would distract from her lovely face . . . I'm just assuming it's lovely. One really couldn't tell from its present condition. Her jaw does not appear to be fractured, but eating may be a challenge for a time. Surprisingly, the only damage to her teeth appears to be a small chip on a lower incisor that shouldn't affect function or aesthetics. I didn't find a wound that required suturing. She could have serious scarring from the whip marks on her back. I'm going to leave a salve that should help some with that."

"What can we do for the pain?" Danna asked.

"I'll leave a few days' supply of laudanum, but I will want to reduce dosage quickly, so I will continue to monitor its use. It is an opiate, and addictive. I have some chloral hydrate . . . sometimes called 'knock-out drops' that we might use for a spell if she cannot sleep after we take her off the laudanum."

Rylee, after remaining silent during most of the treatment, spoke. "My friend, Jael, knows a lot about Comanche medicines. Can she try those?"

Micah hesitated for a moment. "The Indians seem to have many remedies that are very effective. I would only ask that she inform me of anything she is doing and share any successful prescriptions with me. Now, for the sake of Tabitha's modesty, I will allow the two of you to clean her up and get her into some nightclothes. I will leave my salve for you to work into the open wounds. I recommend cold compresses for bruised areas."

Danna and Rylee set promptly to their tasks, and it did not occur to Danna until an hour later that she had left it to Micah to walk the mile to his office. She would have to make it a point to apologize. And it would provide a convenient excuse to see him again.

17

JAEL HAD LEFT at sunrise to ferret out ingredients for her poultice. She found a dozen prospects, including willow bark and cattail roots. She also harvested some peyote buttons from cactus, not for internal consumption, but to provide a pain-killing component for the poultice. She had then visited Dr. Rand to obtain his approval. He seemed surprisingly interested and curious and had taken notes. He saw no reason that the poultice would do any harm.

Jael was convinced she could significantly relieve Tabitha's pain, especially that triggered by the whip lashes. She was confident the wounds could be healed with minimal scarring. She had applied the poultice several hours earlier, and Tabitha seemed to be resting more comfortably within minutes.

The attack had triggered rage among the Rivers family and Tabitha's friends. When Jael and Josh returned the evening of the incident and found Danna and Rylee cleaning the wounds, Jael promptly took command of the nursing care. Josh, after being assured that his sister was not at the brink of death, had departed to find Wolf, who was camping at the site of the new property, where he intended to construct a temporary shelter before winter. When the two men arrived at the house, Wolf had immediately moved to Tabitha's bedside and knelt and taken her hand in his. She had opened her eyes for the first time since Jael's arrival, and a faint smile appeared on her battered face before she dropped off to sleep again.

When Wolf stood, the silent fury Jael saw in his face sent a shiver down her spine. The perpetrators should be praying that Marshal Calder identified and arrested them before Wolf found them. Dr. Rand had said he expected Tabitha to be reasonably lucid in the morning. Josh and Wolf would be present to collect any information that would provide a clue, so they could start their investigation. What baffled them all was motive. Why would anyone launch such an assault on Tabitha?

Now Jael was on her way to locate Moses Monroe. She had been told the old man lived in a room at the Robinson stables, which had not been damaged by the fire.

She had not changed out of her riding britches and moccasins prior to heading for her visit with Monroe, and she still wore the pullover doeskin shirt that had seen a few too many years. She knew she did not look very professional, but she was gambling Monroe might be more open with someone attired less formally.

As she walked down the bricked pathway that led to the stable behind the ruins of the residence, it occurred to her that the fat man who followed her to Luisa Cortes's home would have passed within view of the stable. She wondered if Monroe might have gotten a glimpse of the stalker. The wide door of the stable was open, so she walked into the shadowy building. The door and several windows along the wall let in broken rays of sunshine, and her eyes quickly adjusted to the dimness. She liked the musky smell of horse barns, and as she walked down the alleyway between the two rows of stalls, she admired the eight or ten horses housed there. She also noted the tidiness of the stable and the freshness of the straw. Moses Monroe obviously took pride in his work.

"Howdy, ma'am"

Jael started at the sound of the voice behind her. She turned and saw the rail-thin black man step from the shadows. He had apparently been standing behind a carriage she walked by.

"Sorry if I startled you. These days, a man wants to be darn sure who's coming for a visit. I'm Mose Monroe." His deep, mellifluous voice somehow belied his scarecrow-like appearance.

Jael extended her hand and stepped toward the man, who took her hand with a surprisingly firm grip. She got a closer look at him now. He was a tall man, and a crumpled slouch hat topped a head of snow-white hair. The flesh of his walnut-colored face looked like it had been engraved with bird tracks. She could tell that his deep-set dark eyes were appraising her as well, and she saw nothing the least bit threatening there.

She stepped back. "Mr. Monroe, my name is Jael Rivers, and I would like to speak with you about Judge Robinson."

"I know."

"You do?"

"Luisa told me you would likely be about. Because of what that man tried to do to her, I might be willing to talk a bit. Do you drink coffee?"

"I'm just starting to get a taste for it."

"Follow me down to my quarters."

He led her to the far end of the building and opened the door to a small room that was well lighted with two windows. It was dominated by a large, iron cook stove that no doubt heated the austere room as well. The subdued heat felt welcome on a day that had turned cool. A cot and a small oak table with two straight back chairs made up the furnishings. A cupboard on the wall and a huge trunk on the floor below it seemed to be the only receptacles for his personal belongings. She caught sight of floor-to-ceiling shelves about a yard wide in a darkened corner, all stacked with books.

"Be seated, ma'am. Coffee's hot. I'll be one minute." He plucked two tin cups from the cupboard, placed them on the table, and then picked up the black pot from the stovetop and poured two cups of steaming brew. He pushed one across the table to Jael and sat down, facing her. "Now we can talk."

"Mr. Monroe. I appreciate your willingness to speak with me."

"Call me Mose."

"If you will call me Jael."

"Done."

"Has anybody else spoken with you, Mose . . . about Constanza Robinson's death?"

"Marshal Calder. I didn't tell him all I know."

"Why not?"

"Better be darn careful what you talk about. Look at what could've happened to you and Luisa. And what happened to your husband's sister last night."

"You know about that?"

"Even thick adobe walls have ears in Santa Fe."

"You seem to know a lot about me."

"Your moccasins are Kwahadi-made. You speak Spanish better than most Mexicans. You talk Comanche. You are known among the Comanche as She Who Speaks."

"How do you know all of this?"

"By habit, I listen. Don't talk much. Don't learn when I'm talking." He displayed a smile that Jael figured, in his prime, would have charmed the ladies. Still did, for that matter.

"I gather you know something about Comanche."

"I lived with a band called Wasps, or Quick Stingers, for a dozen years. Had me two wives and three children till the small pox took the children and one wife. The other wife decided I was bad medicine and left me. You were with the Antelope Eaters."

"My people did not like the Wasps. They lived near the settlements and helped the whites against their brothers."

"True enough. Some did. I heard of you through some of my old tribesmen. I was a runaway slave from a Louisiana plantation and headed west around 1854. Comanche captured me but my kinky hair and black skin saved my scalp. Seems they thought I was a buffalo spirit of some kind. When the war ended I came to Santa Fe. I didn't find but a few folks who cared about whether I was a black man, if I didn't get too uppity, so I stayed. Worked for the judge for close to ten years."

"I'd like to hear more of your story another day and, perhaps, share some of mine. But I need your help. I visited with Luisa again and picked up a hint you think Tabitha's beating might be related to Constanza's death."

"Not directly, but I'd wager some of the same folks are pulling strings."

"Who might this be?"

"I don't know exactly which ones. But the League is where I'd be looking. You ask Miss Tabitha Rivers if she's been snooping into the League's business."

"I will. But why do you think the League's involved?"

"Right here's where I got to make a decision." He unfastened the top buttons of his faded flannel shirt and tugged it away from his neck, revealing a line of thick scar tissue encircling his neck. "My price for freedom. Master's wife came to my straw mattress. Master found us buck-naked and entangled. Missus said I dragged her in and raped her. Master didn't believe her, but his pride called for a nigger hanging. They left me for dead. Figured leaving me hanging from a tree for a few days would serve as an example to any that didn't know their places. Thank the Lord, my brother, Joseph, followed and was watching. I had a bull neck in those days, and it hadn't broke. After the master was gone, my brother saw me breathing and cut me down, and I ran till I dropped, and then got up and ran again. Never saw Joseph again. He'd be ten years younger than me, but I don't expect to ever find out what became of him. May be better not knowing."

"You said you have to make a decision."

"Question is, do I want to be the main player at another nigger hanging? These folks would have one in a minute if they saw me as dangerous."

"That's for you to decide. I don't want to be responsible for talking you into something that costs your life."

Mose sipped at his coffee and studied her face appraisingly. She unflinchingly fixed her eyes on his. She feared her interview would be cut short, but she was not going to press him. Besides, he seemed like a man more likely to help if he believed it was truly his choice. Slavery would likely contribute to such outlook.

Finally, Mose spoke. "I should have been dead the day I got this fancy ring around my neck. Bad or good, every day since has been a bonus. I'm not going to get off this earth alive anyhow. Mrs. Robinson always treated me good. Her killer ought to hang, and I don't think it's the judge. Not that the judge doesn't bear some fault."

"Tell me about the League."

"I don't know a thing about the inside workings of the League. I just know it's there. It seems to be kind of an unofficial club of government folks and private thieves who work together to get more than their fair shares of the money Washington sends out this way. Mostly money that's supposed to be used for the Army or the Indians."

"I understand how that can be done. I've seen it already at the Fort Sill Comanche reservation. The cattle herds come in and there is a count taken, and two weeks later half of the allocated beef gets to the Comanche. The remainder of the herd has disappeared. There are any number of ways this can be accomplished. Sometimes, half the herd doesn't make it to the reservation in the first place. The seller gets paid for all, less a commission to the purchasing agent. And the seller sells the remaining cattle again to somebody else who takes actual delivery. There seem to be no auditing controls. Josh says it works so long as nobody talks. He calls it a conspiracy of silence."

"You got it, Jael. Silence. If somebody breaks the code of silence, a scandal breaks out, and it all blows up. Until a new batch of snakes comes along."

"Now tell me where the judge comes in."

"He belongs to the League and wanted out."

"How do you know this?"

"I took the judge places in the carriage. I saw money change hands. I overheard arguments. I'm just an old worn-out black man. I'm invisible. Nobody would guess I'd be interested in what they're talking about, or understand it if I was."

"Are you certain the Judge wanted out? Did you hear him tell somebody that?"

"I heard him tell two men. The first was a man by the name of Simon. I think that's a first name. They always met at night, most always at the old pueblo ruins north of town. Used to get out there once every few weeks, but lately, it had been about every other night."

"Do you know who this Simon was?"

"Does something with the government, I think. Works out of Santa Fe. But I don't think he has an official office he goes to or anything. Got to be a big shot in the League. Maybe the biggest. Anyhow, I heard the judge tell him at least twice he wanted out of whatever they were doing.

The last time . . . maybe a week ago . . . Simon told him that nobody got out alive."

"But you don't know the exact nature of the judge's part in the League?"

"Just know he made lots of money for a judge. Always paid me good. Got me a place to sleep here. I get the leftovers from the kitchen. I'm not a drinking man, so I put away almost everything the judge gave me. I won't go hungry if I lose this job."

"You said there was another man."

"The Reverend Hiram Sibley. He's the preacher for something called the Church of Miracles. Claims to heal folks. Congregation meets at a deserted Spanish mission they've been fixing up. Came here about two years ago and got cozy with the judge right away. The missus was a papist, of course, and the judge joined up with the Catholics when they got married. Didn't go to church with his wife hardly ever, though. Reverend Sibley showed up here at the hacienda to talk to the judge every so often. Left his horse someplace and walked here mostly, but a few times rode in to the stable. A few days before the missus was killed, the reverend met the judge here in the stable. I was sitting right here, sucking up my coffee with the door open. They didn't know I was here."

"What were they talking about?"

"Judge was in tears that day . . . never knew him to cry before. I'd always thought he was made of stone. He was begging the preacher to help him get out of the League. He offered to give five thousand dollars to the Church of Miracles . . . twice my life's savings . . . if the preacher would get him released. Of course, since the preacher is the church, it would have been money he could have done with as he saw fit. Anyway, the preacher said he had no power to help and just told the judge to accept it."

"You seem to have some skepticism about the preacher."

"I think he's in the preaching business to make money. I heard of a blind man who got his sight back after the preacher laid hands on him and prayed. This blind man was a stranger nobody'd seen before and disappeared after the meeting. Same with a crippled girl. He left his horse with me once when he came to visit the judge. I'd been cleaning stalls. It was hot as Hades and I was sweating some. Preacher said he was sorry I had to work so hard to make a living. I said, 'God helps those who help themselves. Chapter Two, Book of Moses.' He looks at me and says, 'a Biblical scholar. Rare in these parts. Good man.' Thought he was going to pat my head like a puppy."

"I was raised Jewish, before I adopted the Comanche Great Spirit, so my education stops with the Old Testament. But I'm sure there is no such Bible verse, and certainly no Book of Moses."

Mose grinned mischievously. "Ought to be, but nope. You would think a real preacher would know that wouldn't you?"

"I'll see what I can find out about these men. I have just a few more questions, and then I won't take any more of your time."

"I got nothing but time since the judge is locked up."

"Did you see the men who tossed the torches through the windows the night Mrs. Robinson was murdered?"

"Not close enough to tell you anything about them. There was three, but all I saw was the rear ends of their horses as they rode off. I was sleeping back here when I heard the commotion. I got up and saw the flames in the house and the dark forms of the riders. Their heads were covered with white sacks . . . like the Klan. I'd never in a hundred years be able to pick any one of them out of a crowd. I can tell you about another man, though."

"Who is that?"

"The fat man you shot dead. I saw him walk by the place that day. He was acting spooked and like he was up to no good, but I didn't see you and didn't know he was following you until I heard gunshots. I'd seen that man before."

"Where?"

"He was with Simon when I drove the judge out to the ruins for some talk. He was there as sort of a watchman, I guess. He was some distance away and wouldn't have heard any talking. But Simon must not have been inclined to come by hisself that night. Last time I took the judge to a meeting with Simon, as I recollect."

"You're certain it was the same man?"

"Hard to miss a feller that big."

"Did you see anybody enter the house the night Mrs. Robinson was killed? Before the fire?"

"Just one person. I was outside taking a piss . . . excuse my crudeness, but that's what I was doing. Do that a lot at night these past few years."

Jael didn't care what he was doing and pushed him back to the story. "Who was it?"

"The U. S. Attorney. Reginald Swayne. Knew who he was because he visited other times when the judge wasn't home. Didn't stay more than five minutes that night. Usually, he visited for an hour or two. Stayed all night a few times when the judge was at the ranch."

This was dynamite. "You would testify to that?"

"I would hate to because it might make the missus look bad. But I've come this far. Yes, ma'am. I would do it."

18

D R. MICAH RAND visited early the next morning and assured Danna and Josh that Tabitha would survive, but he warned she should rest and not to get back to work too quickly. He recommended they continue application of Jael's poultices, admitting he could offer nothing that would be more effective. Tabitha had awakened during Rand's visit, but attempts to speak were garbled and nonsensical. Rand suggested reducing the laudanum significantly to see how she responded. They could always increase it again if she could not tolerate the pain.

Wolf stopped by as the young physician was leaving. Rylee had already left for work at the Second National, and Jael and Michael were in the stable saddling their horses. Jael planned to ride with Michael to the schoolhouse before heading for the Rivers and Sinclair offices.

Danna and Josh were debating who should stay with Tabitha and did not hesitate to accept when Wolf offered his services. Evidently, Jael had an important report that all members of the firm wanted to hear.

Wolf sat in the quiet of Tabitha's room, studying her bruised face, as she slumbered in her drugged sleep. His mind uncovered the damaged flesh and saw the vibrant beauty beneath. He had never loved her more. He knew at that moment whatever trails their lives took, there would never be another he felt this way about. Her spirit would always ride with him, probably to the chagrin of any other woman who might enter his life.

It was midmorning when her eyes opened and she saw him. At first, she seemed confused and disoriented, but then he was relieved to see she recognized him. She reached out her hand and clasped his, and they sat for a time in silence. Finally, Wolf spoke. "You need to eat. There is a coffee pot on the cook stove, and Danna left the ground corn and beans for a porridge. I can make that in no time. Later, we can try some eggs and hotcakes. The doctor said it may be painful for you to chew."

She nodded her head. "I am hungry."

"That I can help with."

When Wolf returned with a pottery cup full of coffee and a bowl of porridge, he set it on the bedside lamp table and helped Tabitha sit up in bed. She groaned only a bit when he lifted her, but he noticed streaks of blood on her flannel gown. Her fingers trembled at first when she tried to eat, so he held the bowl and spooned the contents to her lips. By the time she took her coffee, she could steady the cup with both hands and drink on her own.

After Wolf put the dishes away, he sat down by Tabitha's bed. "Do you need anything for your pain?"

"Not now. And I am not taking anything that muddles my brain. I'm back in charge of my life, and I intend to keep it that way."

"Do you feel like talking about what happened?"

"Yes. And then I am going to write about it."

That statement worried him. "Tell me what you can."

She told him what she remembered about being accosted by the men when she arrived home. Not surprisingly, much of her recollection was hazy, given her semi-consciousness during much of the attack. "I focused on things that might help identify the men. The stocky one gave me the most to work with."

"What do you mean?"

"He was thickly built and carried the Bowie knife. He was the one who wielded the bullwhip. He also had a large circular scar on top of his right hand, like he had been branded with a hot poker. The tops of his hands and wrists were covered with thick, black curly hair. And he spoke with a slight lisp, but you would have to listen for it to notice. He wore fancy black boots. They were tooled with serpents or something."

"You said you don't recall noticing anything about the lookout?"

"No. I was not lucid by the time he showed up. The taller man seemed to be the leader. He had spent too many years in the saddle . . . stooped just a bit."

"That could apply to half of the men in Santa Fe."

"I suppose, but that's the best I can do." She hesitated. "You asked me if I had any idea why they did this, and I didn't answer. I do know, and I had just as well tell you since I've made a decision."

"That sounds ominous," Wolf replied.

"They beat me because I've been investigating the League. I also had a conversation with Reginald Swayne and mentioned the League. He was visibly perturbed."

"I am not clear about who belongs to this so-called League and what they do."

"That's what I am trying to find out. I smell a big story there."

"I gather you are expected to cease your investigation?"

"The tall man said harm would come to a member of my family if a word about the League appeared in the *New Mexican*. I guess he figured he had shown me what they are capable of. I can't back away, though. I can't let those people get by with this. I intend to write an account of what happened to me and what I was threatened with. Can you use a Remington?"

"I carried a Remington carbine for a time during the war."

"Don't be ridiculous. You know what I'm talking about. The typewriter."

"Good Lord, no. I've never touched one and don't care if I ever do. Nothing will ever replace good penmanship."

"You're sounding like an old fogy. I just thought I might be able to tell you what to type. I guess you will just have to help me over to my machine." She nodded toward the typewriter resting on a small table near the window. "Move the chair over there, and then help me get to the chair." She paused, and added, "Please."

With serious reservations about facilitating this stubborn woman's crusade, Wolf put the chair in place and then lifted Tabitha from the bed, savoring her closeness before he placed her in the chair.

"I could have walked with your assistance," Tabitha said.

"Possibly."

"But I didn't mind."

"I trust you are going to discuss this with Josh and Jael before you publish a story mentioning the League. It could be their lives or Michael's at risk . . . even Rylee's."

"Yes, of course, I will do that." She rolled a stiff sheet of paper into the typewriter's carriage, and soon the machine's rhythmic clacking was the only sound in the room.

Wolf left the room and claimed a stuffed chair in the parlor, where he could wait in some comfort and ponder. He could hear easily from this spot if Tabitha called or the typewriter's racket ceased for an extended time. He knew she was hurting because of the beating, but he knew from experience that focus on a task or mission had a way of pushing pain aside for a time. He would remain with her until someone else returned to the house. Then he would commence his search for the stocky attacker. He had no doubt he could learn a great deal from this man. But first, Wolf decided, he would surrender his badge to Marshal Chase Calder.

19

AT JOSH'S REQUEST, Wolf agreed to remain for a time after Jael and Josh arrived to stay with Tabitha. By that time Tabitha had finished writing her story and surrendered to Wolf's insistence that she return to bed. Not surprisingly, Wolf thought, the pain resurfaced with viciousness. Thankfully, Jael moved quickly to prepare and apply fresh poultices, which seemed to have a numbing effect on the raw wounds. She also insisted Tabitha take a very light dose of laudanum, following Dr. Rand's instructions about gradually phasing down the dosages.

Tabitha's eyes started to flutter as the laudanum took hold. "Oliver, tell Josh and Jael about the men and their threat," she mumbled as she slipped away into her drugged sleep.

They left Tabitha in the bedroom and settled into chairs in the parlor, while Wolf repeated Tabitha's story of the attack and the descriptions of the perpetrators. "The worst of it is that they've threatened to harm a family member if she publishes anything that mentions the Santa Fe League. And she has already written a story for the *New Mexican* that will do precisely that. She planned to warn you before the story came out, but she will not be intimidated."

"No," Josh said. "She would not, and should not. We'll keep Michael out of school and with one of us until the threat is over. Jael, will you discuss this with Rylee?"

"Yes, but she will refuse to miss work because of the threat. I suppose she's not as much at risk as you or Michael. Speaking of Rylee, I could have a chat with her boss, Willi Spiegelberg, about the League. He might know something."

"What if he's a member?" Wolf asked.

"I wouldn't believe it even if he claimed to be. First, I trust him without reservation. He's an honest man, and he has a huge distrust of governments. Being complicit with federal officials in a scheme of this sort would be contrary to everything the man believes. Finally, he is Jewish, which makes him an outsider who would not likely be admitted to a cabal of Gentiles."

Wolf said, "After I turn in my badge, I will find the stocky man. He may not know much, but he will tell me what he knows."

Josh's brow furrowed with concern, and Wolf thought the lawyer was going to caution him about tactics, but he evidently thought better of it.

Jael said, "Josh is going to speak with Reverend Hiram Sibley. Do you know him?"

"No. I've heard of him. Church of Miracles. Fixing up the old mission east of town. I've been told he's outdrawing the Presbyterians these days for the non-Roman crowd. Of course, that's still slim pickings here in Santa Fe. He's involved in this some way?"

Jael said, "I am informed he has connections with the League."

"That's an interesting relationship for a preacher."

Josh said, "Interesting enough to warrant a conversation."

20

MARSHAL CALDER WAS noticeably perturbed when Wolf stopped by the courthouse and turned in his badge. Wolf was relieved, however, to be rid of the responsibility. He had construction projects to oversee and had picked up a commission for a portrait of a Spanish don, who had offered a nice sum for a nude painting of his mistress as well. He also was pressed to put up a winter lodge on his recently acquired property. Priority, however, was to locate the animal who had beaten Tabitha.

Now, Wolf was headed for the stables at the Exchange. Almost all Santa Fe equine traffic passed through the stables at one time or another. Wolf stabled his big stallion, Owl, and a dove-gray filly, at the Exchange livery. The filly, tagged Sugar because of a sweet disposition and dusting of white spots on her rump, was breeding age now, and he expected to breed her to Owl to start the foundation for a small herd. He was still haunted by the grisly day he had rescued the two animals from the increasingly infamous slaughter of Comanche horse herds by the Army at Palo Duro Canyon.

Wolf personally checked on his horses several times daily, and he had become quite friendly with Jasper Cox, one of half dozen stable hands who worked in the three horse barns near the hotel. Jasper, a wiry man with a gimpy leg, had arrived in Santa Fe before Mexico ceded the soon-to-be territory to the United States in 1848. He had married a Mexican woman and had built a successful livery business of his own prior to selling out to the Exchange a few years earlier. He had stayed on to feed his addiction to horses, an affliction shared by Wolf.

As he entered the stable where his horses were lodged, Wolf caught sight of the grizzled horseman, pitchfork gripped in his calloused hands, cleaning out one of the stalls. "Jasper," Wolf said, "can you spare a few minutes?"

"Sure enough, Oliver," the old man said, leaning his pitchfork against the wall and limping toward Wolf. "I don't need much of an excuse to jaw a spell when I'm forking horseshit. Love my horses, but I ain't never been attached to cleaning up after them."

"Did you hear about what happened to Tabitha Rivers?"

"I sure did. They say some bastards beat the living hell out of her. I can't imagine. She's purty as a fawn in the forest and sweet as can be. I love that little gal and give her gelding, Smokey, special treats she leaves for him."

"I'm looking for one of the men who attacked her. I'm hoping you can help me find him."

"Don't know what I can do, but I'll sure as hell help you turn up the sumbitch if I can."

"Short, stocky man. Hairy forearms and tops of his hands. Wears fancy boots. Might have serpents tooled on them. Carries a Bowie knife and has a circular, red scar on top of his right hand. He can use a bullwhip. Might talk sometimes with a bit of a lisp."

Cox pushed his dirty slouch hat back from his forehead and was silent for some moments, evidently searching his memory. Wolf waited patiently.

Finally, Cox spoke. "Follow me, Oliver."

Cox hobbled with deliberation to the far end of the stable and stopped next to a stall holding a chestnut-colored gelding. "See the whip scars on the animal's back, even across the muzzle? Owner likes to use a bullwhip if this horse misbehaves."

Wolf seethed at the sight of the abused horse. "You're suggesting this horse might belong to the man I'm looking for?"

"The description fits right down to the Bowie and fancy boots. I saw the scar on his hand. On both sides. I'd guess a bullet went through the hand some years back. The man carries a pistol low on the hip. Fancies hisself a gunslinger, I'd guess. He showed up in town a week or so back. Goes by the name of Lash. Don't know if that's first or last. Probably don't matter, since it's likely made up. Bullwhip's hanging up there on the spike with his tack."

"He came before the judge's fire?"

"Now that you mention it, I guess so. He's not bunking in town. Spends his afternoons and early evenings playing poker at the Silver Palace. Comes by here and picks up the horse just after sunset and rides out. I think he's one of the rough types that beds down out at the new church."

"The Church of Miracles?"

"Yep. More like the Church of Fools, if you ask me. Seems like a strange place to be putting up lowlifes. Of course, I don't know nothing about religion. My Lupe is Roman and the three boys got baptized that way. Never took for me, though."

"What do you think of Reverend Sibley?"

"Not much. Doesn't speak to the likes of me. Got too much money for a man of the cloth, to my notion. Something damn fishy about that operation."

"Could it be tied up with the League?"

That got Jasper Cox's attention. He cocked his head to one side, and his translucent, blue eyes met Wolf's own. "I don't know nothing about no League," he said.

21

WOLF SADDLED OWL and left the stallion in the stall while he eased down on a heavy wooden chest containing bridles, lead ropes, brushes and other supplies. He sat there in the darkness that had just descended, the calming silence broken only by the occasional stomp, snort or whinny. He relished the relaxing interlude and welcomed some peace before he dealt with Mr. Lash.

Thirty minutes later a shadowy figure appeared in the open entryway to the stable. Wolf pulled his black Plainsman hat down on his forehead and tilted his head forward with his chin resting on his chest, feigning sleep as the stocky man staggered past him. He lifted his head slightly after the man made his way to the far end of the stable, where the abused horse was quartered. It was, indeed, his quarry. A little drunk, perhaps, but he would wake him from his stupor soon enough.

Wolf gave Lash time to saddle his horse and ride out of the stable, before he fetched Owl and followed. He was not concerned about losing the man to the dark, moonless night, for he had scouted out the old mission where the Church of Miracles was located and knew exactly where Lash was headed. As soon as they were outside of Santa Fe's town limits, Wolf nudged the stallion forward and began to close the gap. Lash's horse was moving at a slow trot, and its rider seemed oblivious to the fact he was being followed. Wolf reached down and grabbed the wooden handle of the stone-headed, Comanche war club that stuck out from the loose flap of his saddlebags. He urged Owl ahead at a full gallop, and in seconds reached Lash, who turned in his saddle toward the commotion behind him. Lash's face was a mask of confusion just before the club smashed into his broad forehead and launched him off his horse. Wolf left Lash where he had fallen, while he chased down the fallen man's mount.

When he returned, he found Lash motionless on the rocky trail. He hoped he had not killed the man. He dismounted quickly and determined that, while his breathing was labored, the thug was not anywhere near death.

Let the bastard get his sleep. He would need it before the night was over.

The muscular Wolf had little difficulty heaving the unconscious man over the saddle of the abused gelding. He bound the attacker's wrists with rawhide strips, pulled them tight under the horse's belly and anchored them to his ankles on the other side. He tied a short lead rope to the gelding's reins, and soon they hit the trail to the Spiegelberg place he and the Rivers family had purchased together. Until Wolf got a new stable constructed on his parcel, they had agreed to share the barn near the house on the Rivers's tract, and this was his destination. He knew that Josh and Jael would be staying with Tabitha and Danna for another week or so until the property's paperwork was finalized, and, certainly, they would not be showing up tonight.

When they arrived at the stable, Wolf untied his parcel and dragged him inside. Lash was starting to moan and shake his head now, so after dropping him on the dirt floor, Wolf stripped the man naked before he had the sensibilities or strength to resist. Then he tied him to one of the roof support posts in the stable's center, the man's back and pale buttocks facing out and his arms stretched upward by a rope Wolf had tossed over a rafter. Satisfied his captive was going nowhere, he tended to the horses and retrieved Lash's bullwhip. He also lighted the two kerosene lamps he had dropped off earlier.

When he turned his attention back to Lash, he saw that the man was at least semi-conscious now and looking about the stable with obvious puzzlement. Wolf walked up beside his prisoner, so he could examine the man's face and reveal his own. If Wolf chose not to kill him, he wanted the hired gun to see Wolf's face in his nightmares the remainder of his days. Lash's eyes darted from side to side, as if looking for an escape, when they finally locked on Wolf's. He was an ugly man, Wolf thought, his face fleshy and unshaven for a good week, and his thick, black eyebrows met over his pug nose to form a single. It would require some creativity to make him look worse. But Wolf took pride in his own creativity.

"Who are you? What am I doing here?" Lash asked groggily.

"Sorry, Mr. Lash. I ask the questions. You answer. That's how we play this game."

Lash's senses appeared to be reviving rapidly. "I don't know what the hell you're talking about, but if you got a brain at all, you'll be cutting me loose. I know folks."

"Ah, now we're getting somewhere. I want to know these folks, too. Let me show you something."

Wolf held up the coiled bullwhip. "Recognize this?"

Lash's eyes widened in fear. "My bullwhip."

"I know how to use this, too, Mr. Lash. I'm quite proficient. I can make it crack like a rifle to get a horse's attention. I snap bottles off posts for fun. But, until tonight, I've never struck the flesh of man or animal."

"Until tonight? What do you mean?"

"I'll show you." Wolf paced some distance behind the squirming man, who was frantically fighting his bonds. He raised the whip and began twirling it in the air before he cracked the tail and it bit sharply at the man's bare buttocks, drawing a sliver of blood. Lash howled in anguish.

Wolf returned to the hired gun's side. "I'm no longer a virgin. And I rather enjoyed that. Was this your first time, too? This way? I'll bet it was. It won't be our last. But, for now, let's chat."

Tears streamed from Lash's eyes. "I don't want no more of that. Ask your questions."

"Let's start with something easy. What's your real name? I know it's not Lash."

"I just go by Lash, first and last. Birth handle is Henry Lincoln."

"Like the President. I hate to tell you, Mr. Lincoln, I'm sorry about what happened to Abraham, but I fought for the Confederacy. I am no admirer of your cousin."

"Ain't no cousin. I swear. No relation of no kind."

"Well, I guess we'll let that pass. Tell me about the young woman you beat and whipped a few nights ago." Wolf could see the panic spread across the man's face.

"What woman? I never beat no woman. Anybody who says so is a lying son of a bitch."

Wolf walked away and quickly administered two crisscrossed strikes across the man's upper back. Lash's screams echoed off the stable walls, and he could hear the horses hitched outside whinnying nervously. He coiled the bullwhip and returned to Lash. "Now, Mr. Henry Lincoln, I know the truth. I was just testing your level of cooperation. Tell me about the young woman."

Lash, between his sobbing, said, "It wasn't my idea. Waldo was in charge. He said we was to go to this lady and tell her to shut up about some League. I guess she writes stuff for the newspaper. I don't know. Not much for reading."

"Who's Waldo?"

"Friend of mine. Says his last name's Clegg. We work together. Take on jobs as a pair."

"What kind of jobs?"

"Odd jobs. Help folks with special problems."

"Hired guns?"

"Sometimes."

"Beating up young women?"

"Not common. But we hired on to do what the boss told us to."

"The law be damned, I guess?"

Lash did not reply.

"So, your boss told you to give the lady a message. Who is your boss?"

"No. Can't say. I'm a dead man if I do."

"You're a dead man if you don't."

"What do you mean? You kill me, and you'll hang."

Wolf returned to his position and attacked with vicious, repeated lashings this time, letting loose his anger at the brutality that had been directed at Tabitha and the horse outside. He could not remember knowing such rage before and felt shame when he finally stopped. He saw that Lash had passed out again and was hanging by his hands, slumped against the post to which he was bound. He pulled a bucket from a spike on a wall and went outside to pump some water. When he returned, he tossed the contents on Lash, who came back quickly enough, but was groaning and sniffling.

"No more," Lash said. "The only boss I know is Preacher Sibley. He gives the orders to Waldo and me. I think he gets the word from somebody higher up."

Wolf decided to run a bluff. "Did Sibley tell you to burn down the judge's house?"

"I don't know nothing about that." His eyes fixed on Wolf's fingers tightening on the grip of the whip. "Okay. Yeah, that was Sibley's orders. Waldo was in charge, but he didn't ride with us. Billy was in on it . . . don't know his last name. He was the lookout the night we went to the lady's house. He took off after that night. Think he decided things was getting too hot."

"There was another man."

"That would have been Pork. He's dead. Got shot by some woman. He rode with us."

"Where's Waldo?"

"He'd be at the preacher's church. We bunk in a room off the church building."

"Anything else I should know?"

"I don't know nothing else. I swear to God I'd tell you if I did."

Wolf picked up another strip of rawhide from the floor and then slammed Slash's head against the post, wrapped the strip around his neck and cinched it tightly to the post, leaving hired gun's head virtually immovable.

The terrified face was angled toward Wolf, who slipped his skinning knife from its sheath. It was regularly honed to razor sharpness. "I'm not going to kill you," he said.

"Then let me go," Lash gasped.

"I will, but first I have to give you something to remember me by. I thought first, I'd turn you around and see if I could slice your pecker off with the bullwhip."

"Oh God, no."

"But my gentleness got the best of me. I'm going to untie you in a minute, and I'm going to let you take that poor horse of yours and get the hell out of here. Go where you want. Back to the preacher if it suits you. Tell him the devil's risen from hell and coming for him. But you're leaving here without your clothes and your weapons, and I'm keeping this whip as a souvenir."

Like a cat attacking a mouse, Wolf snatched Lash's left upper eyelid and peeled it off with his knife blade. A sheet of blood covered the eyeball simultaneously with Slash's screams. Wolf spoke softly, "That's for Tabby."

22

DANNA HAD INVITED Martin Locke and Jael to meet with her in the conference room to discuss the Robinson case. A pot of coffee and a plate of ginger cookies sat in the middle of the splintered and scarred table.

Pouring herself a mug of steaming, black coffee, Danna mused, "I think we could afford a new conference table. This thing looks like a butcher block, and you can't write on it without punching holes in your paper. I'll have to stop at Spiegelbergs' to see what they've got."

Jael said, "If you're looking for something special, I suspect Oliver Wolf could craft something for the same money."

"That's a thought. And we do owe Oliver something for the information he has provided, although I don't think he's hurting for business. I'll have to speak with him." She paused, thinking she should have run when Judge Robinson asked her to represent him in the criminal case. She hated this type of work, and she did not think she was particularly competent as a defense lawyer. She would ask to withdraw as counsel if Marty were not available to manage the case behind the scenes. "Well, we can't put this off, there are decisions to be made. The judge has been sitting in the U. S. Marshal's jail for a week now, and he is not happy about it. Marty, any thoughts?"

"The trial date's not set yet. The man's charged with first degree murder, and Judge Cooper denied bond. We have a client who's hiding something and won't help us. I think he's afraid. He's stuck, unless we make some breakthrough that would warrant Swayne dismissing the case or reducing the charges. The evidence is mostly circumstantial, but we need an alternate theory of the murder to establish reasonable doubt."

Danna said, "It seems probable the fires were set at the direction of someone connected with the League. I think Oliver has learned that much, but any testimony on his part is hearsay or speculation. I am baffled why Oliver did not bring in the man who beat Tabby. His testimony might have helped point to a murder conspiracy by another party."

Jael said, "I think Oliver may have secured his information in a manner that would make the man's testimony deniable in a courtroom . . . and it might cause problems for Oliver."

"What did he do to the man?"

"I don't know, and I'm not asking."

Danna said, "It all comes back to the so-called League. We might have been able to smoke somebody out if the *Daily New Mexican* had not refused to print Tabby's story."

"The news editor refuses to print the story until the publisher returns from back east in a few weeks," Jael said. "Tabby thinks the publisher will sign off on it, but she suspects the news editor, Edmund Thorne, is on the League's payroll. She's worried now that she jeopardized her family's safety by submitting the story. Needless to say, she's ready to kill Mr. Thorne."

"Please," Marty interjected, "no more killings. One murder charge at a time to defend is quite enough. But how is Tabitha physically?"

"She's doing well," Jael replied. "She moves a bit stiffly yet, but her wounds are healing nicely. Her face is bruised, but no longer swollen. She refuses to go in to the newspaper until Ansel Jackman returns, so she's working on her books and helping Oliver build his lodge.

It's not really a tipi like the Comanche live in. It's less roomy and shaped more like a dome, but I'm sure he knows what he's doing and it should be cozy this winter. He'll start building his house and studio in the spring, he says. Josh and Michael are with them, getting our house ready for us to move into next week. Josh has work here at the office to get done, but we feel one of us needs to be with Michael at all times until we know there is no more threat to the family."

Danna said, "Josh tried to talk to Sibley, but, so far, the man hasn't been found at the church. Oliver doesn't want to interfere with our case, but he has offered to visit with Reverend Sibley. He believes the man is an important link to the League, and that's consistent with what Jael learned from Moses Monroe. Oliver says he will speak with the reverend eventually, regardless, but he will defer if we want to interview."

"Under the circumstances," Marty said, "Jael should stay away from this self-ordained preacher. She's a part of the Rivers family. But I think someone from the firm should talk to the man before Oliver does. My sense is that Oliver's priority is not the judge's defense. I would be willing to approach the man."

Danna said, "Jael needs to spend a few days studying, and she can do some research on a land title case I have. I would like to take on Reverend Sibley. Marty, I think you should talk man-to-man, so to speak, with Judge Robinson. He's not playing straight with us. Maybe he will tell you something he is uncomfortable telling a woman. We have nothing to lose."

"I'm concerned about your safety," Marty said, "if you ride out to the Church of Miracles on your own."

"He will know that others are aware of my visit. He won't try anything while I'm there. Besides, I won't go unarmed. You can ask Josh about it sometime. I killed a man in a church once."

23

L EVI RIVERS SWUNG into the saddle and eased the skittish bay gelding through the corral gate. The horse was tagged with the name, Spook, for good reason. The five-year-old had always been a nervous animal and not as reliable as some horses on the Slash R, so he was not the first chosen from the remuda for work chores by the cowhands. Levi had unexplained sympathy for the horse, though, and picked him out of the cow horses from time to time. Besides, his favorite, gentle Nell, a buckskin mare, had recently foaled, producing a look-alike buckskin filly he hoped to give to Michael when the time was right.

Nell was a younger, full sister to Buck, Josh's beloved gelding that had been killed during a buffalo hunt when Levi's lawyer son was recovering Michael from the Comanche. He hoped Michael would spend part of the next summer at the ranch and get to know the filly. She'd be easier to break then, when the time came.

He was getting ready to ride out, when he saw Dawn come out of the house and hurry toward the corral. The striking, auburn-haired woman, a dozen years younger than his sixty-eight, had made life fun again. She was a stoic and generally quiet woman, but she had a playful side she rarely revealed to those who knew her only casually. And she had become his best friend. He treasured the time they shared, the simple touch of a hand when they sat, side by side, reading on the settee in the parlor, the inviting caress under covers in the night.

"Levi," Dawn said, as she approached, "I couldn't let you ride out without asking one more time. Wait till Nate and the hands get back tonight and talk it over with your son before you take off for Cimarron. Nate's your partner in the Slash R. He should be a part of this anyway."

"Jed Duvall's message said he had to leave for Denver in three days, and he thought I should swing west and look at the land before I meet him in Cimarron. I know where it connects to our place, but I never thought we'd have a chance to buy that ten thousand acres, so I never checked the grazing prospects. Beautiful mountain country to look at from a distance, but I don't know about the grass and water. Got to know that before we talk money. Besides, Nate manages the cow herds without me sticking my nose in. We've always understood that adding to the land was my bailiwick."

"I wouldn't worry, but that letter we got from Josh about the threat to harm someone in the family concerns me. That young man who rode in with the message from Duvall last night seemed nice enough, but we don't if he's who he said he was."

"He said he was Duvall's nephew. He could have left the message without saying he's related. I'll be fine. Don't worry."

"I love you, Levi, even if you can be a stubborn old coot. You come home safe, and I'll make it worth your while."

"With an offer like that, there's no way I wouldn't show up. I love you, Dawn Rivers. I won't be gone more than four nights. Tell Nate to be thinking about expanding the cow herd."

He leaned his head down, and she stood on her tiptoes to kiss him. Then he pointed the bay west and they moved out at a brisk gallop. As he rode across the lush valley floor he observed the grass was turning from a carpet of emerald that covered the earth just a month ago to drab shades of brown as winter approached. It also reminded him that despite the mountain sun warming his back this morning, sundown would bring on an unpleasant chill. He wore a sheepskin vest and had an old mackinaw wrapped up in his bedroll, which included a bulky buffalo robe. He did not relish nights on the ground these days—Dawn had spoiled him for that—but he had always had an aversion to cold. He had no doubt forgot some things, but his weapons against the cold would not be among them.

When the sun was midway on its own westward journey, Levi dismounted near the bank of Big Goat Creek, the stream he had been following, and dug some hardtack from his saddlebags. Coffee would have been nice, but he did not want to take the time to build a fire and make some. That would have to wait until night camp when he could open a can of beans to sop the hardtack in. He would indulge in a few of the apple-chunk cookies Dawn had sent along, too. A man should have cookies with his coffee.

Levi's eyes followed the clear, swift-flowing stream as it formed a ribbon of water splitting the Slash R range and snaked its way down from the imposing Sangre de Christo Mountains into the valleys below. The land he wanted to check out commenced at the base on the mountain range, and he wanted to find the nooks and crannies that might offer decent grazing.

His banker son, Hamilton, had pointed out that lumbering prospects should be considered on some of the Slash R's mountain property where grazing was sparse. Ham had noted that the Slash R was within a day's journey to the mountain branch of the Santa Fe Trail that ran northward through Cimarron and Raton Pass into southern Colorado, where increasing settlement was creating a demand for lumber. And Santa Fe offered a viable market. Ham was currently engaged in a partnership with his brother, Cal, establishing a Denver to Santa Fe freighter business, which conveniently would be able to expand to timber hauling.

Ham knew how to make a dollar, and his ventures almost always cranked out returns to the investors. Maybe he should listen to Ham's suggestions. It would be nice if the ranching operation were not always subject to the whims of the cattle market and the weather. He would have to watch the rascal, though. Ham would not be above taking more than a fair share from his father and elder brother, and Levi and Cal had something of a contentious relationship.

As hoped, Levi reached the foothills by dusk and built a good fire and set up camp before darkness crept down the mountainside. After eating his beans and hardtack, he sat down on his buffalo robe, as near as he could to the fire without getting scorched, and savored his coffee and cookies. He stared dreamily into the fire, remembering the days he first came to this part of the country from south Texas, and how he had been captured by the solitude and the contrast of semi-desert and rich grass and timbered mountains that thrived in such proximity to each other. Where was this thing men called heaven, if not right here?

Then he looked up toward the mountains and saw the rider on the ridge, silhouetted against the moonlight. Levi scooted back from the firelight. The man was probably a hundred fifty yards away, but there was no doubt he could see the fire from his vantage point. If he intended no harm, he would ride in close and dismount, and, then, with hands in clear sight, lead his horse into the camp.

Instead, the rider turned his horse away and disappeared into the night. Levi got up, rubbing the gimpy leg that tended to stiffen with the night chill. He had put up with it since he'd taken a tumble and been stomped by the last wild horse he'd tried to break a dozen years earlier. Some things were best left to the young and senseless, he decided after the incompetent splinting of the broken limb.

Levi turned his thoughts back to the ghostly stranger. It could have been a coincidence—another rider who simply wasn't looking for company this night. More likely, it was an Indian hunting for game, who was merely curious about who was sharing the foothills this time of day. If he did not speak passable English, a fresh cup of coffee would not have been worth the clumsy conversation. Levi had a hunch he was avoiding reality. His gut told him the rider signaled trouble on the horizon.

He picked up his bedroll and moved it into a clump of trees some distance from the fire. He retrieved Spook and tethered him closer to the campsite. The horse was so damned goosey, he would be better than a watchdog if a troublemaker lurked about. So much for keeping warm tonight.

24

L EVI CRAWLED OUT from under his buffalo robe after enduring a sleepless night. Spook had been too much of a watchdog, whinnying nervously at the rustle of grass triggered by a gust of wind or the chirping of a finch or the croaking of a tree frog. Now he had to decide. Make a run for home? Continue his appraisal of the Duvall tract? And now he found himself sharing Dawn's doubts about the legitimacy of what had become the alleged Duvall message.

He decided in favor of a cup of coffee while he considered the matter. He was not hiding from anybody. The rider, if he was stalking Levi, knew exactly where to find him, so Levi lay some twigs over the near-dead embers of the previous night's fire, and, with some huffing and puffing, blew life into it again. He was not in a mood for hardtack, so he depleted the apple-chunk cookies as he drank his coffee.

After he ate, he made up his mind to allow two hours to ride into the Duvall property. If it interested him, he would ride due east and could still hit the mountain branch of the Santa Fe Trail before nightfall and likely find the company of travelers there. Tomorrow he could be in Cimarron to take care of business. If he did not consider the property a good investment, he would hightail it back along Big Goat Creek and be home before dark. Meanwhile, he would watch his back and stay out of the open as much as possible.

After Levi tied the bedroll behind the saddle, he checked his Navy Colt revolver to confirm that the weapon was fire-ready and levered a cartridge into his Winchester's chamber. Then, he mounted Spook and nudged the horse toward a deer trail that appeared to wind through the foothills and into the mountains. Less than two hours later, they had worked their way to a rugged promontory that overlooked what he calculated was the Duvall tract. The view was breathtaking. There were several broad valleys that dovetailed into an outlet that connected to Slash R grazing land. There was a lot of waste from a cattleman's viewpoint, but not so much so if he also wore a logger's hat. If he could purchase the land at grazing price, he just might talk to Ham about the logging business.

Levi did not even hear the crack of the rifle before the bullet drove into the side of his forehead, and he felt nothing when Spook reared and spilled him on the rocks. And he did not see the frightened horse racing frantically down the trail and stumbling on treacherous footing before coming up lame and slowing the pace of its descent.

25

TABITHA FOUND HERSELF enjoying the work outdoors with Wolf as he constructed a winter lodge. She had donned the doeskin britches and shirt she had worn during her weeks in Quanah's village. She had even slipped into the well-worn moccasins, wondering why she had surrendered their comfort to the tight, inflexible city shoes she wore with her dresses to the newspaper. It occurred to her she had established her career well enough that she could now choose to write wherever she desired. She had earned her right to make choices,

She knew she was safe here with Oliver. Between the two of them, they could fight off an army of thugs. She was confident of that. Her strength had returned, and the whip cuts had healed nicely, leaving only a residue of soreness on one shoulder where the whip's tongue had dug deeply. She accepted that the scar there would always remain as a remembrance. With Oliver's guidance, she had learned how to lash the poles to form the framework for the lodge. The design of the structure was not much different than the Comanche tipi they had shared for a month the previous winter. It was just more compact and less spacious, rounded on the top instead of conical. They had started stitching the skins over the bent poles when they arrived this morning, and they were nearly half completed before they started the afternoon. Oliver hoped to have the shell completed before they returned to town, and it appeared they would accomplish the task with time to spare.

Working with Oliver reminded her of the time they had shared caring for the starving Comanche before that last trek to the reservation. They spoke little, but she took great comfort in his physical presence, and she knew he was pleased to have her with him. She knew also that he loved her, but she resisted giving him the opportunity to say the words. A man was not a part of her plans. And still she loved watching him move about their little camp, his body lean, yet thickly muscled, like a cougar male in his prime. Once again, as she thought about that time, she could not imagine now how they had remained chaste those days and nights they shared a tipi. It was more a tribute to the Cherokee's self-discipline than to her own, she decided. She could never have denied him if he had approached her and sought to share her robe. The image warmed her now and shot a wave of hunger through her body that unnerved her.

Wolf startled her when he spoke. "Josh waved when he and Michael left at noon. Are they coming back?"

"I don't think so. They were going to rent a buckboard and pick up some furnishings at Spiegelbergs'. Then, they'll drive it into the stable at Danna's and my place, and Jael will come out with them in the morning to help unload. I volunteered our help. I hope it's okay."

He displayed a rare smile. "Your brother warned me you'd take charge of my life if I let you."

She could feel her cheeks blush. "I know I can be a little bossy. You'll have to remind me if it bothers you."

"I will. Why don't we take a break? Coffee pot's brewing on the coals. We've been working hard for three days now. We've about won the battle, so there's no reason we can't slow down a little." He tossed a few small logs on the fire and spread out a buffalo robe. He signaled her to sit down and then poured her coffee in a tin cup and handed it to her. After he poured his own, he joined her.

"Fire feels good," Tabitha said. "There's a chill in the air. I don't notice it when we're moving."

"The mountains to the north will be getting snow within the next few days. I really haven't wintered here, but I don't think we'll see so much."

"We won't, but Pop will be seeing more than he wants. Sometimes he comes to Santa Fe for a few months in the winter. I wasn't here, but I guess he stayed at the ranch last year. Maybe with Dawn there, he's happy to hole up during the storms. After Mom was killed and I went off to school, I imagine winters got pretty lonely for him."

"But your brother and his family are there."

"Yes, but they've got their own house a mile away. Nice, big log house. Usually, the ranch homes are in kind of a compound, but I think Nate's wife, Julia, needed a little distance from Mom. I loved my mother, but she always had her own ideas about what was best for everybody else. Maybe it's because she used to be a school teacher. She taught all the kids at the ranch, even included the few that belonged to the ranch hands. She tolerated no laziness, and Pop couldn't pull the boys away to work when school was in session."

"I guess you were lucky she was a teacher. I suppose you lived miles from any school."

"That's true. And when I went to Denver to college, I didn't have any catching up to do."

"Well, your folks taught their kids about work. You've really made a difference on this project. It was good of you to help."

"You've helped me more than I can say, since the beating. You stopped every day. You made me feel attractive when I must have been the ugliest woman in New Mexico. Besides, I've loved being out here with you. And I'm envious of this property you and Josh bought. I'm excited to see the house and studio you're going to build. When are you going to move out here?"

"Tomorrow."

"Are you serious?"

"Yes. I've already got most of my tools and art supplies stored in Josh's barn. He's got room for my two horses there until I get something up next spring. And I need to get out of the Exchange Hotel."

Tabitha's mood darkened. She was very aware of who else lived at the Exchange, and she hated the jealousy that crept into her mind at the thought of Oliver with Jessica Chandler. Personally, she liked Jessica and admired the woman's talents. She felt like a witch when she asked, "Does Jessica Chandler have something to do with it?"

In his typically blunt fashion, Wolf replied, "Yes. She has a great deal to do with it. I was seeing Jessica, but we have agreed to settle for friendship."

Tabitha did not want to know just how much of Jessica he was seeing. "I understand. I suppose it's still awkward living in the same hotel and encountering each other all the time."

"Probably more difficult for me than Jessica. She seems to be quite casual about her romances."

Promiscuous would be more like it, Tabitha thought, but she held her tongue. "Well, now you can turn the page to the next chapter of your life, whatever that is."

"Yes, whatever that is."

Damn him. Why didn't he say something about Oliver and Tabby? She decided to change the subject. "Oliver, Jael told me you found one of the men who beat me. Why didn't you say something?"

"There's nothing to say. I found him."

"But you didn't have him arrested?"

"I wasn't certain you could identify him. And there was the complication of the threats on your family."

"So, you just let him go?"

"No."

"Well, then what happened?"

"We had a discussion. He confessed. He may be dead now."

"You killed him?"

"No, but someone else may have. I promise he paid for his crime. Don't force me to give you the details. You cannot write about it. Trust me. He was the man with the whip. I now have the whip in the stable. He regretted his part in your beating."

There truly were times to walk away from a story, and she decided this was one of those times. "I guess I have enough to write about, and I'll find more. I've got more words in my head than I'll ever be able to write."

Wolf startled her by reaching over and taking her hand in his. She turned her head toward him, and their eyes locked. "Tabby," he said, his voice soft. "I've kicked myself repeatedly for not speaking my feelings when we were with the Comanche. You are not going to cut me short this time."

Part of her did not want him to say what she felt he was going to say, but she found herself speechless.

He continued. "I think we are both at a crossroads. You can forge straight ahead, and I take one of the turns. We are both the kind of persons who will make our lives productive and good if we go our separate ways. But I want us to take the same road and see where it takes us. I love you. I can't ever clear my mind of your lovely face, and your impish smile, and even that exasperated, pouty-lipped look you get. My happiest moments are when I'm with you, and most of those moments have been spent working side by side. I can only imagine what laughing and playing together would be like."

This quiet man had taken her breath away with his words. "I don't know what to say. Is this a proposal of marriage?"

"Only if you want it to be."

"I had decided my life was not going to include marriage, that there wouldn't be room for it. I will not live my life for another person, and I will not expect another to live his life for me. But I love you, Oliver, as I've never loved any man. I'm not sure about the commitment of marriage. Perhaps we could carve out our own kind of marriage in the future—circumstances might dictate that. But I don't want us to be apart like we have been these past months. I'm willing to start down the same road with you and see where it takes us."

He leaned over and kissed her, and her lips lingered on his for a moment before she responded hungrily. After that, she was aware of his touching and caressing, and of being lifted from the earth and carried into the lodge shell. Somehow the buffalo robe ended up with them, and they lay naked together on it, exploring each other tentatively and gently. Finally, when she thought she could wait no longer, he moved to her, and she raked her fingers down his muscular back, as she commenced her journey to ecstasy, grateful Oliver Wolf was traveling with her.

26

TABITHA AND WOLF worked out details for their living arrangements, which would have been scandalous in many Eastern towns and eyebrow-raising in some of the rural communities of the West, but worth only a feeble yawn in Santa Fe. Until the house was built—which would now include an office for Tabitha—Wolf would live in the primitive lodge and work at his various construction commitments on site. His art projects would continue at the town workplace he had rented temporarily until he could move everything to what they now dubbed "the pueblo" for the Navajo look that would rise from the naked landscape.

Because there was no writing workspace presently on the premises, Tabitha would continue to reside and work at the residence she owned with Danna until new quarters were available. She promised her overnight vis-

its would be frequent. Ultimately, they would each contribute funds for living costs to a joint account from time
to time but would otherwise keep their assets separate.
Tabitha, because of her publishing contracts and copyrights, had prospects of significant wealth, but the en-
terprising Wolf was unconcerned about being labeled
a "kept man." He was confident he could contribute his
financial share to their lives, and Tabitha's love, he figured, made him the richest man in Santa Fe.

Tabitha was a wild mix of the spontaneous and me-
thodical, Wolf decided. They had made precise plans for
their living arrangements, but several days after Wolf's
affirmation of his love, Tabitha was still spending nights
with him at the lodge, and he was not about to object. "I
like supper here," she told him. "Danna and I can't cook
worth a damn."

"You can leave after supper," he teased.

"And miss the dessert I brought?" she responded with
feigned incredulity.

Josh's family had moved most of their belongings to
the nearby residence yesterday, and Jael, who had shared
a tipi with Tabitha in Quanah's village for just short of a
year, told Wolf she was thrilled at the prospect of having her friend as a neighbor whenever she and Josh were
in Santa Fe. Tabitha obviously shared Jael's enthusiasm

about the reunion as well. Wolf was perplexed about the nature of female friendships. There seemed to be an emotional, less superficial, connection between some women that was rarely found in male friendships, he observed. Loner that he had always been, he supposed he was not much of a judge of such things.

Wolf and Tabitha sat at the fire eating a venison and potato stew he had concocted. Tabitha had brought some soda crackers she picked up at Spiegelbergs' before she left town, and they went nicely with the stew. It was not yet sundown, and from the direction of Santa Fe, Wolf could make out a small cyclone of dust headed their way. Somebody was riding fast and hard. As the dust cloud neared, he saw it was Josh riding his recently-acquired, red-roan gelding, a young, powerfully-built horse, far from the late Buck's match, but a promising beast nonetheless.

He expected Josh to head for the stable, but, instead, he veered toward the lodge. When he dismounted, the grim look on the law wrangler's face warned Wolf that Josh was not making a social visit. Wolf and Tabitha put their bowls aside and got up to greet her brother.

"Josh, there's something wrong. What is it?" Tabitha asked.

He handed her an envelope. "The kid from the messenger service brought this to me at the office. He said it was dropped in their message box with a silver dollar and a note to tell me to get the envelope to you, before somebody else dies."

"Somebody else? What does that mean?" Tabitha said, taking the envelope and tearing it open. "You could have opened this, you know. I wouldn't have cared."

"Not comfortable doing that."

She unfolded the sheet she pulled from the envelope and read aloud. "About the time you read this, Levi Rivers will be ready for his funeral. You chose not to do what you were told. Pull the story now or others will join your father."

"They must have sent someone to kill Pop," Josh said.

"Oh, my God," Tabitha said in a near whisper. "What have I done?"

"It may not be too late," Josh said. "I've got to get to the Slash R."

"It will take two days at least. It will be too late."

"This could be a stunt to scare you off. Even if it's not, there is a chance that any attempt to kill Pop will be unsuccessful," Josh said. "We alerted all the family. I'm sure he's being cautious."

"Pop, cautious? Since when?"

Wolf let the siblings talk themselves out of words before he spoke. "I can leave tonight. Owl is in good shape for a ride, and Sugar can keep up easily. Switching horses, I can be there tomorrow night or, at the latest, the next morning."

"We can't expect you to do that," Josh said.

"I'm going with you. You've never been to the Slash R, and I know some shortcuts." Tabitha said, "Smokey's rested, and Josh, you can loan me an extra horse. You should be sure your own family's protected before you leave. You can make whatever arrangements you need, and then you can follow tomorrow."

Tabitha had a point, Wolf thought. He could travel faster alone and was certain he could find the place with directions, but his unfamiliarity with the area would slow him down some.

"Okay," Josh said, "you're right. I think it's time to report the threats to the U. S. Marshal. You know him, Oliver. Can he be trusted?"

"Yes. His hands may be tied by the prosecutor and other politicians, but I'd bet my life on Chance Calder."

"You may be doing just that. Anyway, I can discuss the threats. He knows Tabby was beaten, but we never made a formal complaint, and he doesn't know why. I can discuss this with him without talking about how it might be related to the judge's defense. He will likely be miffed he wasn't given the story earlier, and I don't blame him. I'll talk to him first thing in the morning and then head for the Slash R."

27

JOSH TOLD JAEL and Rylee about the message Tabitha received. Then he went to Michael's bedroom and explained to his son that he would be gone for a time to visit the Slash R.

"Take me with you, Dad. I want to see Grandpop and Grandma Dawn, and I've never been to the Slash R. Grandpop asked if I could visit for a month next summer."

"You can do that next summer. But I must make this trip alone. You have to stay here to look after Mom and Rylee."

He gave a pouty-lipped protest and quickly returned to the dime Western novel he was reading. He loved the stories, although he found the Comanche stories hilarious, having spent the larger part of his years as a Comanche himself. Josh was pleased with the boy's reading progress. Thankfully, Jael had insisted he master English from the moment he learned to talk, and when Tabitha joined them as a captive reporter, both women had worked with him on reading and writing skills. Josh did not care much what he was reading at age seven, so long as he was developing a hunger for the printed word. He recalled he had read somewhere once that "words are the parents of thought." Those thoughts, in turn, Josh believed, open the gates to knowledge.

Josh just hoped the boy would have the opportunity to know Pop. They had hit it off when grandfather and grandson reunited at Fort Sill after the boy's return to the white world. Levi and Dawn had visited Josh and Jael's Fort Sill home a month after the Comanche surrender, and it had been the first occasion Josh could remember seeing his father cry. And Josh had always thought the crusty rancher was devoid of emotion. He had also been taken aback when Levi hugged him and said, "I love you, son."

Josh had always been secure in the knowledge of his parents' love, but to hear Levi verbalize it struck him deeply. And he realized at that moment, he did not really know the real Levi Rivers. He had vowed he would take the time to do that, but, of course, he had not. And now that opportunity might be lost forever.

Josh returned to the parlor where he could see Jael and Rylee were plotting. He did not delude himself that he would dictate a strategy for their protection. They had faced more danger together on the Staked Plains than the League could serve up. But he wanted to hear what they had in mind.

Jael looked up when he entered the room, her dark eyes searching his. Why had it taken him so long to realize how much he loved this woman? He would be forever grateful that his captive son had ended up in her care. "Would you ladies like my opinion on anything?" he asked.

"Your opinion is always welcome, my husband. But, perhaps, you would like to hear our thinking first."

"I'm listening."

"Rylee thinks we should return to Danna and Tabby's house during your absence. We are too isolated here, and there is too much distance to our work. We should avoid being alone. Michael will go to work with me. I will speak with his teacher, and he can work on his lessons in the conference room. Rylee will pick up some more of his novels at Spiegelbergs' to keep him otherwise occupied."

"He has adapted to civilization quickly, hasn't he?"

"This is what you call civilization?"

"Okay. Withdraw the question."

Rylee intervened. "We will go to work together and come home together. We will ride, not walk. And take our rifles with us. Of course, Jael always carries a Colt or Derringer in her pocket book. I will have my .44 Russian."

"I have no other thoughts."

Jael said, "Josh, the threat to the family ends when the League is exposed. There is little doubt the League has something to do with Judge Robinson's situation. I do not know if he is guilty of his wife's murder or not, and I understand the firm has the responsibility to defend him regardless. But there appears to be no chance of helping him without bringing the League to public attention. I do not think our firm has any conflict with Tabby's efforts. We can help each other."

"I agree."

"Then I hope Danna will permit me to do more work on this case."

"That is for the two of you to work out."

"I receive no help from the senior partner?"

"None."

28

L EVI FOUND HIMSELF sprawled, face-down, near the edge of the promontory when he regained a foggy and dizzy consciousness. Another yard in the wrong direction and he would have plummeted into the abyss below. Hammering jolts of pain wracked his skull, and when he tried to sit up, nausea and vertigo overwhelmed him and forced him back down. With trembling fingers, he probed his forehead and felt the wet, slick blood that painted it. An enormous lump protruded above his right eye. It appeared to be centered by a cratered open wound. Bullet hole? Was he alive?

He must have been shot. Spook was gone, of course. So was his bedroll and rifle. He felt his hip. At least he had the six-gun. Some bastard had taken him down. Good shot. He should be dead, if he wasn't. He had no idea where the shot came from. Then it occurred to him that the bushwhacker would likely confirm his kill, and that thought sparked some clarity. He had no clue how long he had been out. He lifted himself up on his elbows and looked around. He was at the high point of the granite outcropping. He couldn't stand, but he supposed he could roll.

He caught sight of the deer or goat trail he had followed to the observation point and focused on the pine and brush that lined it. After an aborted effort to get up, he started rolling down the slope, gaining momentum until his body was abruptly braked by the brush. He lay on his back for some moments, collecting his thoughts, and then rolled over and dragged himself a dozen feet into the forest. He found himself in a cluster of aspen trees and picked one of the sturdier-looking and inched his back up against it. The dizziness came on again, but he refused to go down and sat there, resting against the tree with his head between his knees.

He did not know how much time had passed, but he was alerted by the rustling of leaves and branches and the intermittent cracking of dead branches as someone—or something—came up the trail. The intruder was either over-confident or stupid, Levi thought. Sometimes, the line between the two was thin. Levi saw movement through the screen of his sparse cover and made out the form of a man, trailed by a big bay. If the visitor looked his way, it was over for one of them, most likely Levi Rivers.

He pulled his pistol from its holster and rested it across his lap, watching with blurry eyes as the man moved upon the rock overhang where Levi had gone down. The horse was further back, evidently having been hitched to a tree branch, while the rider went ahead on foot. He could see the man kneeling where Levi had fallen and then look his way. The blood. Of course, he had left a trail of blood. The would-be killer stood and drew his pistol, which was slung low on the hip. This guy considered himself a gunfighter. He started walking toward Levi's tree, eyes cast downward, as he followed the victim's advertising. When he broke into the forest, Levi, surprised at the effort it took to speak, said, "Drop your gun and raise your hands, or you're a dead man."

The gun dropped and the hands went up, but the man took several more steps in Levi's direction before he saw the man with the voice. "I'll be damned, old man. The way you went down, I didn't think there was a chance in hell you'd be alive."

"You're the young man who brought the message. You claimed to be Jed Duvall's nephew. Lying bastard."

"No lie. I am Jed's nephew, Tobe Duvall. And my uncle wants to sell. But he didn't send no message. Some friends in Santa Fe hired me to take you down. Looks like I made a good hit. Your head's just too damned hard. But you're going to die. I can see that."

"You're just a kid. Can't be more than twenty. You're a fool to waste your life like this."

"I get a thousand dollars when I take your left ear back. My friends say you got a notch in it, just like an old bull that's been marked."

The kid was right. A Comanche arrow had clipped the ear years ago when Levi first tried ranching in Texas. "You've got to finish killing me first, boy."

"I'll just sit down and wait for you to die or pass out. You're going to be dead as a can of corned beef in a short time. Men like you don't shoot an unarmed man. At least you'd do the fair thing and give me a chance to draw."

Levi squeezed the trigger once, and the explosion roared in his aching head. Then he pulled it again, confident he had driven two slugs into the young man's chest. "You're wrong," he said, before he passed out again.

When he awakened, he guessed from the sun's location, it was just past mid-afternoon. It was the warmest now that it would be this day, and he didn't like the looks of the clouds brewing up in the west. His mind seemed clearer, but the throbbing in his skull had not abated any, and it seemed his body had the strength of a rag doll. He first sought out the would-be killer's horse. Gone. He supposed it had torn loose upon hearing the gunfire and followed Spook's example. Still, he held out hope the animal might wander back this way.

He studied the body of the young gunslinger which lay less than fifteen feet from him. He found himself saddened, but not sorry. Young Duvall wore a wool, hip-length jacket that could be salvaged and might be useful. It was bloodied, but so was everything else. Levi would see if the Stetson that lay nearby might fit. His own had disappeared, possibly over the edge of the precipice.

He found he still could not stand up for more than a few seconds, so he crawled over to the body and clumsily began stripping it of clothing, including shirt and trousers. He could not explain why, but, after some struggle, he pulled the fine boots back on the naked man's feet. The coat felt good against the wind that was stirring up. He wrapped the remaining garments in a bundle. He had been pleased to find some matches in Duvall's pocket, as well as a pocket knife that was better than his own. He assumed the five gold eagles were a down payment on Levi Rivers's life.

Next, he needed to find shelter as close to the trail as he could get. If he recovered enough to walk, he did not want to lose the trail, because he could find his way to Big Goat Creek once he got into the foothills. Also, in the unlikely event somebody came looking for him up this way, he did not want to be hidden in the maze of the forest. Duvall's remains should be evidence of his passing this way.

He grabbed a branch of a tree and pulled himself up. He staggered a few paces and went to his knees. Okay, he would crawl for now. He maneuvered himself deeper into the woods, gazing upward toward a tier of rock rising above him, hoping he might ferret out a cave or fissure in the rock for shelter. He saw nothing promising. Then, as he stretched a hand forward to obtain new purchase on the earth, he struck air. He scooted ahead on his belly and hung his head over the brink of a dry arroyo winding its way through the mountain ridge, likely carved by eons of gully-washer rains. He had not seen it because it was well concealed from his vantage point by a ceiling of overhanging ponderosa and cedar branches from the trees that lined the side.

It appeared to be about four feet deep at this point and about the same width at the floor, somewhat narrower as it extended to higher ground, wider as it dropped. The area below him seemed reasonably level. He dragged his legs around and slid down the sloping mix of crusty soil and rocks. When he landed on the bottom and looked up, he could not see the sky through the shield of branches. He did not have the strength to climb out, and the wind didn't strike him here. He was too tired to wait for nightfall. He just wanted to sleep. If he was meant to die here, so be it. He rolled up Duvall's shirt and britches to form a crude pillow. As he lay his head down, it occurred to him that the bleeding from his wound had stopped.

It was nearly sundown when he heard Aurelie's voice. "Wake up, you old fool."

His eyes opened with a start, and he moved his head slowly from side to side, seeking the source of the voice. "Aurelie? Am I dead?"

"You will be soon enough if you don't get a fire started."

The voice seemed to be coming from his own head. But then he saw her, sitting on the ground in front of him, her legs tucked back under the tattered gingham dress. It was the same garment that had been found next to her naked body after the Comanche finished with her. She was looking at him sternly with lips pressed tightly, the same expression she had shown frequently ever since he showed up at the ranch with baby Tabby some twenty-three years earlier. Suddenly, her image disappeared, and he could not say he was sorry. Enough of his sensibilities had returned to convince him he had been hallucinating, but the vision and the voice had been too real for his comfort.

Regardless, he did need to do something about a fire. He brushed his fingers against his face. It was burning. Not good. He touched the swollen wound above his eye. There had to be a lead slug imbedded there. He had miraculously survived the impact, but he knew if the object was not removed, the wound would putrefy, and a slow and tortured death would visit. He struggled to lift himself up, so he could sit and test his strength. He leaned back against the wall of the arroyo. The pain in his skull might have faded some, but, on the other hand, perhaps he was building a certain tolerance for it. The dizziness persisted, and he did not think he could walk upright.

He scrutinized his surroundings. There was a good supply of scattered dead limbs on the arroyo floor in both directions, and the forest would yield more if he could climb out of the pit he had claimed for his residence and retrieve it.

On hands and knees, he spent the next hour gathering up a wood supply. Then he took the confiscated pocket knife and reduced some of the sticks to wood shavings and tinder. With a shaky hand, he struck one of his matches on a stone. The flame died before it reached the fire nest. The second effort succeeded, and soon he welcomed a healthy blaze. He cherished the small victory and barely noticed the smoke that was unable to filter through the coniferous branches overhead and bounced back to form a gray haze about him.

Then, an urgent thirst struck, along with the realization he could survive some days without food, but water was another matter. But he was exhausted and needed to rest just a moment. He lay back down, and dropped into a deep and fevered sleep.

Aurelie woke him up rudely. "You're on your death trail, Mister, if you don't get up."

And there she sat looking just like she had before—sour, grim-faced, and pissed. Until that last day, she had remained a pretty woman when she smiled. Hard work had kept her trim and firm, and she could still turn the head of men of a certain age. He had still wanted her, but he only succeeded when her guard was down, and that was rare. Still, he had loved her to the last day, at least in the way he understood love then.

Blackness cloaked the mountains now, and a gray mass floated overhead to block the moonlight. Snow on its way. Exactly what he needed. "I'm thirsty as hell," he told Aurelie. "Got to find water."

"Won't find it sitting on your butt."

He managed to sit up with less hassle this time, and his head felt clearer. Why in the hell wouldn't she go away? But she was right, he needed to get moving. As his eyes adjusted to the darkness, he considered the crisis of the moment. He had no container for water if he found it. He thought about it a spell. His boots would hold water. He wished now he had scavenged the boots from the man he killed. If the snow came, he could dump snow in his boots and place them near the fire to melt the snow. It would be a tedious process, but it might work. He would have to ignore his thirst till morning. It made no sense to crawl and stumble around in the darkness. Chances of coming across a stream or spring before daylight were next to nothing.

"I can melt snow in my boots," he told Aurelie. "If it doesn't snow, I'll see what I find in the morning."

"I guess that will have to do. In the meantime, we need to talk about Tabitha."

29

DANNA STOPPED BY Dr. Micah Rand's office. She had thought of something she wanted to ask him about Constanza's death before she visited the Church of Miracles. His assistant informed her he was not in and that he was busy with an autopsy at Spiegelbergs' funeral parlor. She said Danna could visit with him there, if she wished, adding that Dr. Rand spoke very highly of her and would likely enjoy seeing her, if Danna would not be repulsed by the setting.

Alfred greeted her at the parlor and nodded in the direction of the embalming room. Micah looked up from the corpse he was probing on the table. He instantly greeted her with the boyish smile she found so endearing and with his scalpel signaled for her to join him. She saw then that the specimen was a stocky, hairy man whose body bore whip slashes and bruises not unlike those endured by Tabitha.

"Do you recognize him?" Micah asked.

"No. I don't recall ever seeing him."

"He suffered a great deal before he died. Look at his eye."

"My God, that is bizarre."

"Someone sliced off his upper eyelid."

"Why would they do that?"

Micha shrugged. "Punishment? Revenge? Sadism? Who knows?"

"It would take some twisted thinking to do this to someone."

"I saw worse when I was an Army surgeon. Folks seem to have an unlimited vocabulary of atrocities to impose upon their fellow man." He paused. "But I want you to see something else." He held up the cadaver's hand.

"A circular scar on top of his hand."

"It's on the palm, also. Something, a bullet or some other object passed through the hand. It's an old wound."

"This is the man who beat and whipped Tabby."

"I should say so, yes."

Suddenly, Danna did not find herself so offended by the torturing of the victim. She recognized that her perspective had changed. "What killed him?"

"A bullet in the brain. Entry from the back of his head. What we sometimes call an execution-style wound. He was found by a Navajo boy walking to town. You can see the buzzards had just started. It was off the trail some distance, and the birds attracted the young Indian's attention. Another day and evidence of most of the wounds, except for the bullet hole, would have been obliterated."

Wolf had a part in this, she thought, but she doubted if he fired the shot that killed the man. That did not seem like his style somehow. He would have killed the man face to face. "I actually came here because I have a question to ask you."

"I have one for you. Supper tonight?"

"You pick the strangest places to ask a lady out."

"I suppose this does not stimulate one's appetite."

"Never mind. Yes, supper would be nice. I'll be working late at the office. Just stop by when you are finished with your work day."

"I will do that. Probably after seven o'clock."

"Back to my question."

"Yes, what is it?"

"When you examined Constanza's body, you discovered five or six stab wounds. I don't recall that you mentioned any other wounds. I was curious as to whether there was any sign of resistance, or if she was likely attacked while sleeping."

"There were no other wounds. If she had been awake, it is true you would expect other defensive wounds on her hands or arms. Her nudity suggests she may have been sleeping or disrobed for . . . a lover. The marshal said there was blood on the bedsheets, although the bed was crushed by a falling ceiling, so the attack must have at least started there."

"So she could have fallen asleep next to a lover, who struck after she fell asleep."

"Or the killer entered the room and found her sleeping. The multiple wounds might suggest this was a crime of passion or extreme anger."

"Either way, I guess there is nothing here that would exonerate my client."

30

THE CHURCH OF Miracles rose from the dusty, pancake terrain like a great Sphinx on a desert. Danna had not anticipated such an imposing structure, having understood that Hiram Sibley had founded his church at the site of a crumbling, abandoned Spanish mission. Serious funds and man hours of labor had been invested here. Sibley's religion business must be prospering, she figured.

She drove her one-horse buggy into the churchyard. She hated riding side saddle, and a woman wearing a long dress astride a horse probably did not suit a lawyer's professional image. Knowing that the other party's perception was no small part of success or failure, she conceded to the buggy.

She reined the horse in near a hitching post and sat in the buggy, surveying the complex. And it was a complex, with the spired adobe church at the center, newly-constructed stables nearby, and an assortment of other structures. She guessed several of the buildings might be warehouses and there was at least one bunkhouse, she guessed. No more than fifty yards behind the church she could make out a crew of workers putting up the frame of another large building. Then she caught sight of a smaller building nestled up to the side of the church structure, and evidently connecting to it. A sign posted in front said, "Office." Its appearance was more that of a commercial structure than a pastor's workplace, but she decided this was the logical starting place. She stepped out of the buggy, hitched the horse, and, bag in hand, walked with purpose down the bricked path toward the office building.

When she reached the structure, she hesitated, uncertain whether to knock or just walk in. She chose the latter and opened the door and stepped in. A full-bearded man, leaning back in a swivel chair with his booted feet propped on the desk and a cigarette dangling from his lips, looked up with mild astonishment.

"Ma'am?" he asked.

"My name is Danna Sinclair. I am looking for Reverend Sibley."

"You found him, ma'am. To what do I owe this pleasure?" He lifted his feet off the desk and stood up, snuffing the cigarette in an onyx ash tray. He was a trim man of average height, several inches shorter than herself, and nattily dressed in a black suit and string tie. His beard was neatly trimmed. He was decidedly younger than she had expected, probably a year or two on either side of forty.

"I am a lawyer from Santa Fe representing Judge Andrew Robinson. I would like to ask you some questions that might help with the defense of charges that have been filed against him."

She could feel the man's eyes running the length of her body. It annoyed her, but she gave him time for his appraisal. She was not above tolerating a bit of long distance lechery to procure answers she wanted.

"Questions?" he said. "I cannot imagine how I might be helpful." He moved around the desk and pulled back a straight-backed chair and gestured for her to be seated. Then he reached for the door and slipped the deadbolt in place. "So we will not be interrupted," he explained.

Sibley returned to his own chair and sat down, staring at her with piercing eyes. She had obviously claimed his full attention. Danna tugged her satchel onto her lap, so the Derringer would be within easy reach. "I don't think this will take long, Reverend Sibley. Your name has come up in various inquiries we have made regarding the case, and, quite frankly, your name has never been mentioned in our discussions with the defendant. We feel a responsibility to track any rumors."

"And what might these rumors be?"

"That you have some connection with an informal organization called the League, and that the judge belonged to the League and desired to disassociate himself from its activities. It has been suggested that Mrs. Robinson's death, and the fire, might have been a warning to Judge Robinson from the League."

"This all sounds like a grand fairy tale. I've never heard of the League and certainly have never had any involvement with such an organization. I would have neither the interest nor the time. My ministry is very demanding."

"Are you acquainted with the judge?"

"I may have met him a time or two at public functions, but I have never had more than a casual conversation with the man."

"Did you know a man by the name of Henry Lincoln?"

Sibley preened his neatly-trimmed black beard and furrowed his brow. "Lincoln? Relation of the President?"

"No. A common woman beater. He generally answered to the name of Lash."

"Ah, I do recall Lash. We have lodging for the destitute here as a part of our mission. I believe he was passing through and stayed over a few nights. He seemed to be a troubled man but didn't respond to my offers of help."

"I have it on good authority that he was one of the men who beat and threatened Tabitha Rivers. He said that you employed him to do that."

Sibley was unflappable. "If he did, he was deranged. I did nothing of the sort. I have no interest in this Miss Rivers, and I know nothing of this League you are rambling on about. You will have to put this Henry Lincoln under oath in a courtroom, and see if he will perjure himself with these ridiculous allegations."

"He is dead, Reverend Sibley. Murdered."

"How unfortunate," Sibley said without emotion. "Now, Miss Sinclair, I am a busy man. You will have to excuse me." He stood and escorted her to the door.

31

JUDGE ROBINSON WAS incarcerated in a barred cell set off from the other five multi-prisoner cells in the complex attached to the U. S. Marshal's office. Usually, the cell was used for the rare female accused or a prisoner who might be a danger to other prisoners. In this instance, it was the judge who was being protected. Any judge or other representative of the law could be at risk if housed among the general jail population. Personal experiences to be avenged were always a possibility, and the hardened criminals tended to despise any representative of law and order.

Judge Robinson sat on a wood-framed cot that was cushioned by a thin, straw-filled mattress. Martin Locke sat down, facing the judge, on a crude chair fashioned from splintery pine. The judge looked sickly, Marty thought. His eyes were bloodshot, and his face was pale and wan, his thinning hair disheveled. He was in his early forties, but he appeared a dozen years older this morning,

"What are you doing here? I hired Miss Sinclair as my lawyer."

Marty had decided that the judge would receive no deference today. Enough of the dance. "The retainer agreement says you employed the firm. Miss Sinclair remains in charge of the case, but she felt you have not been forthcoming with her and asked that I meet with you this morning. I am the firm's designated trial lawyer, and I will be very involved in your defense. If that displeases you, we will be more than willing to withdraw from the case and allow you to engage more congenial counsel."

"You're an impudent bastard, aren't you? Very well, proceed with whatever you wish to talk about."

"I have questions. And I need answers. Otherwise, you are going to climb the golden stairs on a rope."

"There's not close to enough evidence to hang me."

"You do not know. It can be established you quarreled with your wife that night and that you returned to the house the evening she died. We don't know what other evidence the U. S. Attorney has. He does not have to disclose at this stage of the proceedings, and he will not."

"Ask your damn questions. I'll answer if I can."

"Is there anyone who can furnish you with an alibi for the night of Constanza's murder?"

The judge sighed. "A partial alibi, perhaps. I wasn't entirely truthful when I told you earlier that I was alone in my room. There was someone else."

"Who?"

"Carly from Eve's Garden."

"The bordello?"

"Yes, Madam Eve sends her to me whenever I message her. Young, pretty, Mexican girl. Speaks no English as far as I know. I use her exclusively. A bit more discreet to, uh, consort with only one. I have to consider my position."

"I suppose," Marty said, wondering immediately about the credibility of the witness. "Was she with you the entire evening?"

"We had supper in the room, and she stayed the night. She left before sunrise, always does."

"But someone will testify she saw you at the hacienda."

He shrugged. "I guess you will have to find out what Carly says."

"We have a clerk who speaks Spanish fluently. I will have her interview Carly, and Eve, too. Any objection?"

"I guess not. This could be most embarrassing if the testimony has to be used during the trial."

"You are charged with murder. Your life is at stake, Judge. You should be beyond embarrassment at this point."

"I suppose."

"Did you know your wife was pregnant?"

"Yes, she told me earlier that day."

"Did you return to the house that evening? You will not be testifying, but we need to be prepared to address that."

"No, I did not. I was with Carly."

"Interesting. This makes me more curious about what Carly will say. Of course, I cannot allow her to knowingly perjure herself. Luisa, the maid, will testify that you came to the hacienda and she overheard an argument. She is very credible, I am told. Next question. You implied that you were not the father of the baby. I assume you have a reason to think this. Could you explain?"

The Judge sighed. "Constanza and I had not been intimate for over five months. We had separate bedrooms."

"You obviously had ongoing differences then?"

"Yes, and I knew she was not celibate during this separation. Frankly, she would have been incapable of it. She had sluttish ways I found inappropriate for a woman of class. And, as I've already told you, I found comfort elsewhere."

"Did you know her lover?"

"Some months ago, young Juan Castillo of the restaurant family was a frequent visitor when I was absent from the house, I was informed. That stopped after I spoke with his father, I believe. I suspected there were others, and that was confirmed by her pregnancy."

"What if I told you the U.S . Attorney, Reginald Swayne, was one of her lovers."

That got the judge's attention, and he raised his head and straightened his shoulders and stared at Marty in disbelief. "You are serious, aren't you?"

"I am serious. Luisa would testify she saw him visit multiple times."

"Then, that would put him on the suspect list . . . one of the seeds for reasonable doubt. Why would he be fool enough to prosecute me?"

"I can think of two. First, he is confident no other person has any knowledge of his relationship with Constanza. He would not have asked Luisa or any other household servant such a question in his interviews . . . if he has spoken with them personally. He could not approach the question of lovers without the risk of hearing things he might not want to hear. Of course, that's very foolish, because, as you know, a lawyer generally should not ask a witness in a courtroom a question he does not already know the answer to."

"You said there was another reason."

"Someone else is pulling strings, and he is the puppet."

"I don't understand."

"The League."

The judge paled. "I do not know what you are talking about."

"Judge, I am not here to play games. I am going to lay it all out for you. We know that you have been aligned in some way with this association called the League, which is evidently engaged in certain illegal activities to the profit of its members. You wanted out, but members don't escape alive. The burning of your house was a message. I am not certain about the murder of Constanza. That seems extreme for a warning, with too many possibilities for unintended consequences. Tabitha Rivers was beaten for investigating the League, and there is a possibility her father has been killed because of it. The members are obviously starting to panic. The Pandora's box has been opened. They are trying to close it, but they will not. It is just a question of how many die before they give up."

"They won't give up. There is too much money at stake and the likelihood that many of the members would face criminal charges. The noose might await some."

"Then you admit to involvement with the League."

"I admit nothing. And I am not going to discuss this further with you. Our conversation is ended for the day."

"Then I will leave you with something to ponder. I have no doubt you know a great deal about the League. They would love to see you hang, but they cannot take the chance of waiting for that to happen. You will not make it to the gallows. You may be innocent of Constanza's murder, but the death sentence has been rendered. You can get a reprieve only by breaking the League."

"I must think about this."

"Before I depart, Judge, I need something else from you."

"What?"

"A few hair specimens. And not from your head."

32

FLUFFY SNOWFLAKES DRIFTED, like goose down, from the starless sky now, starting to dust a white cloak on the ground about him. His roof of overhanging branches was filtering out most of the snowfall, but it could not ward off the chill that had resulted from a sudden, noticeable temperature drop. Levi tossed a few more logs on the fire and moved closer to the blaze. The pain raged in his skull, and his fingertips told him the swelling about his wound was growing and beginning to cause a lump of flesh to droop over his eye. He curled up in a fetal position on the rocky earth, confused and exhausted. Several hours later, he awakened or thought he did. He wasn't certain.

He felt her presence, but it did not particularly unnerve him. In a way, he welcomed the company. He sat up. Yes, Aurelie had returned, and she was facing him across the dying embers, sitting on the opposite side of the narrow arroyo. "What do you want now?" he asked.

"We were going to talk about Tabitha and then you passed out."

"You were going to talk about Tabby, not me."

"It's time."

"For what?"

"It's time for her to know."

He knew what she was talking about, but he asked anyway. "Know what?"

"That she had another mother before me."

"It doesn't matter. You're the only one she's ever known. She's happy enough with that."

"Nate and Hamilton know. They were twelve and ten when you brought her home. They remember. Josh and Calvin were six and five, and just seemed to accept the new baby as a surprise. They probably never gave it much thought."

"Nate and Ham would never say anything."

"Can you be certain they haven't told their wives? And what about her mother's family? Some know. Sooner or later it will slip out. Do you really want her to hear from somebody else? Of course, it's probably too late, since odds are you're going to die up here."

She disappeared before he could respond. But she had left him thinking. Levi and Aurelie had shared a tumultuous marriage, but he supposed that was true with lots of folks, and people just found their own ways of dealing with it. In Levi's case, he had found his way in Taos. Summer had been bright and warm as the season for which she was named. She was the daughter of a trader there, a widowed white man who had been married to a full-blood Navajo woman. Summer, some twenty-five years younger than Levi, worked in her father's trading post, and that was where he met her.

Her father had warned her to stay away from the married rancher when he thought Levi was making too many contrived trips to the store and lingering too long with Summer at the counter. It was too late, and the daughter was as spirited as a wild horse, and would not have listened anyway. She was also smart as a whip, Levi remembered, and devised countless ways for the couple to rendezvous. One thing led to another, and Summer was soon carrying Levi's child.

When Levi returned to Taos after spring round-up that year, he had been absent for nearly two months and learned only after his arrival that Summer was five months pregnant. Furthermore, Summer had been disowned by her father and was now living with her mother's sister in her pueblo quarters, but the few small rooms were crammed with children and other relatives. Levi found a single-room adobe house in town and arranged a line of credit for Summer at the store of her father's competitor. He also located a Navajo midwife, who would check in on Summer from time to time and help with delivery of the baby when the time came.

This had been one of the few times in his life when he had known panic. He would never abandon his financial responsibility for Summer and the child. He was still captivated by the young woman who neither demanded nor expected anything of him. His passion for her was undimmed, and he thought at the time it was love. But love withstands trials and tests, he understood now, and they were never confronted with the reality of decisions to be made together and the consequences of the path they might have taken.

Summer died just minutes after their baby daughter was born. Levi was there, holding her hand, when she took her final breath. And he sobbed while he cradled the baby in his arms. The midwife found a wet nurse at the pueblo, a woman who had recently given birth to her own child and agreed to nurse a second baby for a spell. Then, he returned to the Slash R to face Aurelie.

Now she was sitting at the fire again.

"I knew something was going on. You were heading down to Taos with stupid, feeble excuses. We would have a little fuss and off you went for a week or more. The foreman and I were left to run the ranch. I figured you were up to no good. But I thought you were bedding whores or drinking yourself blind . . . or both."

Oh, God. The woman was back. "I can't say anything to justify what I did, Aurelie. I never did. You know that. I never expected forgiveness, and I sure as hell never got it."

"When you told me what you'd done, I wanted to turn you into a steer before I killed you."

"I could tell. I've never been as scared since as I was that night I told you about Tabby."

"But I told you to bring her home."

"Yes, and I loved you for that. It took a special kind of woman to take that child in."

"I would have done the same for an orphan calf. And much as I despised you for what you did, I couldn't turn away my boys' baby sister. I resented the little waif at first, and there were times when I wished you would take her and go. But I came to love her, and most of the time I forgot she wasn't my blood."

"But she became yours. She never knew another mother."

"I suppose, but her tawny skin and dark eyes were a constant reminder another woman gave birth to her. And she was always her papa's girl, like she knew her blood bond was with you. You taught her to shoot and ride and work cattle. You bragged she could outride any hand on the place. She was a wild thing. Never wanted to be in the house working on her schooling if she could be with her papa."

"But despite all that, you saw to her book learning and gave her the love for words that took her where she is today. That didn't come from me, and she credits you for that."

"She went off to school like I wanted. I won that battle. I feared we'd never get her off the ranch, and she'd fuss with Nate over running the place. I know you would've sided with her. She always got her way with you. Could do no wrong."

"Not worth arguing about. It turned out fine. And all of our kids are something to be proud of . . . even that wrong-headed Calvin."

"You ought to tell him."

"You've got all kinds of ideas about what I ought to tell folks."

"You've been a hard man where the boys are concerned. We had our troubles, but there was a time when

I saw a warm and gentle side to you. I guess you showed it to that half-breed woman, but neither I nor the boys saw it after you brought Tabby home. She got to see that side but nobody else did. Time for you to change that."

"I think I've had about all your advice I can take. I'm tired. Let me sleep."

"You go to sleep and you're not going to wake up. Snow's piling up. You need to keep that fire going. You got to have water. Of course, you're likely going to die anyway."

"Could be. I guess we'll know soon enough."

He had started fading away again during the conversation, or maybe he was already asleep, and it all had been a dream. Perhaps she had found a way to crawl into his aching head, but she appeared to have taken off for now. His dizziness had eased some, and his senses were perking up. It was near sunrise, he guessed, but he was not going to see the sun anytime soon. The darkness outside his shelter had turned gray from the huge white snowflakes that were dropping like an avalanche from the sky. In case anybody came looking for him, any trail he had left behind would be covered. He fed the fire some more sticks and observed he needed to add more to his stack before the snow buried all the fuel from his sight.

But first, the water. He grabbed a boot, leaned out from under his coniferous roof and began scooping up snow to melt, realizing it would take many hours to maintain a water supply in this fashion. But he might survive a while longer. He'd be damned if Aurelie was going to be right this time.

33

WOLF AND TABITHA had taken the mountain branch of the Santa Fe trail and rode most of the night, stopping to rest occasionally, and switching horses from time to time. When they reached Big Goat Creek, which marked the cutoff to the trail that led to the Slash R, they still faced a six-hour ride, Tabitha informed Wolf. The horses had been pushed to the limit, so they setup a cold camp next to the stream, a mile off the Santa Fe Trail. After staking out the horses where they could access the stream and have decent grazing, they shared some hardtack and deer jerky, and then Tabitha and Wolf crawled into Wolf's bedroll. She snuggled near him, savoring his closeness, and he tossed an arm over her waist and spooned up against her back. They both fell instantly asleep.

Four hours later, they were in their saddles again. As they rode, side by side, Tabitha admired Wolf's grace in the saddle. His supple form moved with the big stallion as if they were one, like the fabled Centaur—half man and half horse. He might ride as well as herself, she thought, not given to modesty when it came to her riding skills. But Smokey, fast as he was, could never outrace Owl. Now, if she could ride Sugar, the filly, Tabitha figured they could leave the males in the dust.

"Somebody headed this way," Wolf called.

They started reining in their mounts, and Tabitha instinctively placed her hand on the stock of her Henry rifle as she watched the cloud of dust move toward them. "Rider's in a hurry," she said.

"Seems to be."

The rider slowed the pace of his horse as he approached. Tabitha relaxed when she recognized the wind-burned, leathery face of Irish O'Gara, a seasoned cowhand who had been with Levi since she was a toddler.

He eased his horse up close and then tipped his battered Stetson. "Miss Tabby. I was just heading for Santa Fe to find you and Josh . . . if he's there."

"He was. He should be a half day behind us. Irish, this is my friend, Oliver Wolf. Oliver, this is Irish O'Gara. Irish is like an uncle to me."

Wolf inched his big stallion ahead and reached out to shake the stocky cowboy's hand. "You can call me 'Wolf,' if you like."

"Pleased to meet you, Wolf."

Tabitha cut the introductions short. "Tell me what's happened to Pop."

The cowhand furrowed his brow. "How'd you know? We just learned last night."

She was getting impatient now. "Learned what?"

"His horse came back last night without him. Your dad rode out to look at the Duvall land. Thought he had a chance to buy it. Spook . . . his name says it all . . . showed up riderless at the ranch two and a half days later. I figured the fool horse threw him someplace, but Miss Dawn insists he rode into a trap. Your brother, Nate, agrees, and he's headed out with his boy, Eli, to look for your dad. Nate knows cattle better than anyone in this part of the country, but intending no disrespect, he ain't no tracker. It'll be dumb luck if he finds anything."

"Aren't there others searching?" Tabitha asked.

"The seasonal hands are all done for the year. That just leaves three of us. Miss Dawn sent me to Santa Fe to tell you and Josh. Figured if Josh wasn't there, a wire could be sent to Fort Sill. Lefty took off to Cal's place, and Lute headed north to find the first telegraph to notify Ham in Denver. Last we knew, Cimarron didn't have nothing working yet and neither does Taos to the south."

Wolf said, "Then we'd better get moving. Irish, you only have one horse. You should give that gelding a good rest. A dead horse won't help anybody. And grab yourself some shuteye while you're at it. We'll go on to the ranch."

Tabitha said, "There will be plenty for you to do when you get back. It sounds like Dawn's got the whole ranch on her shoulders right now."

Wolf's stallion lunged forward and quickly eased into a fast gallop, leaving Tabitha spitting dust. After the dust cleared, she trailed after him, urging Smokey to catch up. When she pulled even, they settled into a rhythmic gait together. She called to Wolf, "Show off."

He smiled back, and she could not summon up any anger. Instead, she found herself wishing they could take a rest and give Adonis the opportunity to ravage her. She wondered if she had turned into a hopeless slut.

When they arrived at the log ranch house several hours before dusk, Dawn and Nate's wife, Julie, met them on the porch. Julie's younger children, Levi II and Katherine, sat soberly and wide-eyed on a bench. Their thirteen-year-old brother, Eli, had ridden out with Nate to search for their missing grandfather.

Tabitha dismounted, and, after exchanging hugs with the two women, introduced Wolf. She noted that Dawn's face was lined with worry, but she seemed otherwise calm and composed. Her blonde sister-in-law seemed unchanged. In her mid-thirties, Julie's face seemed undamaged by the havoc usually wreaked by the mountain sun and rugged ranch life. She was not a flashy woman, but she was regally attractive and always poised. Her inner calm was with her today.

They entered the house and sat down at the large dining table. Tabitha could see that Wolf had slipped into reticence, deferring to Tabitha to carry the conversation.

"Dawn, we met Irish on the cut-off trail. He told us about Pop's horse coming back to the ranch. We were on our way here because I received a message that the men who had me beaten in Santa Fe were going to carry out their threat against Pop. I had no way to send a warning, so we came as quickly as we could. Josh won't be far behind. What can you tell us about this?"

Dawn told them about the message Levi supposedly received from Duvall about the sale of ten thousand acres, explaining that Levi planned to check out the land and then meet Duvall in Cimarron. "I tried to talk him out of going, especially alone, but he can be headstrong sometimes."

"Stubborn as a jackass is more apt," Tabitha said. "Where is this place?"

"I don't know for certain, but one reason he was interested was because Big Goat Creek passes through it. He said that would link it nicely to the main ranch and protect the Slash R from somebody damming up the stream further up and cutting off the best water source for the ranch."

"So some of this must be mountain acres?"

"Mountains and valleys. He was thinking of getting into the lumber business if there wasn't enough grass to warrant Duvall's price. I gather he wanted this land badly."

"Ranchers aren't land hungry. They just want the land next to them," Tabitha said with a tinge of sarcasm.

Wolf broke his silence. "When did he leave?"

"Three mornings ago. He's been out three nights. This will be the fourth"

"When did the horse return?"

"Last night."

"What about his rifle and bedroll?"

"With the horse."

Tabitha said, "We'd better leave tonight. Where was Nate heading?"

Julia, who had been silent during the exchange, said, "He planned to follow the creek. It seemed like the only thing we knew for certain. Eventually, that leads to the Duvall land, from what we've been told. There is something that has not been mentioned, though."

"What's that?" Tabitha asked.

"It cleared off today, but from the clouds covering the mountains, it's a good bet there has been some serious snow in the high country. I hope he didn't get that far, whatever happened."

Wolf said, "We'll need fresh horses. We've pushed ours to the limit. If you folks could put together some simple edibles for us to take along, it would be appreciated. We'll want to pack some blankets or buffalo robes on one of the spare horses. Whenever Josh or Irish show up, I'd like one of them to hitch a team to a buckboard and follow the creek as far as they can. I don't know this country, so I'm not certain how far you can take a wagon."

"Till you reach the foothills," Tabitha said.

"One other thing," Wolf said, "do you have any snowshoes?"

Julia said, "Nate's got his hanging in the barn. Levi's are there, and there are a few extra pair. I'll gather them up for you."

"I'd like to get on the trail within the next hour."

34

JAEL AND DANNA relaxed on the settee, and Michael had dropped off to sleep on the bear rug in front of the fireplace. Rylee sat in the rocker, catching the flickering light of a kerosene lamp from the nearby table, while she was engrossed in the new novel by Louisa May Alcott, *A Rose in Bloom*. A perfect evening, Jael thought, if only Josh were here to share it. They had busy lives that carried them separate ways during their work days, but she missed him terribly when they were apart at night. They could live to be "ancient ones," as her Comanche friends called the very old, but they would never share enough nights together. Until it happened to her, she never believed it was possible to love any man with the intensity she felt for Josh. Sometimes, it made her uneasy that her life could be so good these days, knowing that it could all change in an instant. Occasionally, she was struck with pangs of guilt from the remembrance that those she considered her people were not sharing her fate.

"You're somewhere else tonight, aren't you?" Danna said, breaking the long silence.

Jael turned to her. "I am with Josh and with my people."

"I understand. Do you mind if we discuss some business . . . the Judge Robinson case, specifically? It's so difficult to get an opportunity to talk during a busy work day."

Jael smiled. "Josh swears your work day never ends."

Danna shrugged. "I suppose I can't deny that. I am a bit driven."

Jael reached over and grasped her hand. "We are what we are. If our nature drives us to achievement and knowledge, we should not deny it, or we will be less than we could be."

"I will have to think on that. Is that a quote?"

"Quanah Parker, Principal Chief of the Comanche. Now, what business did you wish to discuss with me?"

"I have another task for you. An interview that calls on your Spanish fluency again."

"I suppose in Santa Fe there is not much demand for my Yiddish."

"Hardly. I want you to speak with a prostitute."

Jael's eyes brightened and traces of a smile crossed her lips. "This might be interesting. What am I to learn from this woman?"

"Her name is Carly. Judge Robinson claims he spent the night with her the evening Constanza was murdered. If he did, that provides an alibi."

"But Luisa will testify he returned to the house."

"Perhaps she was mistaken. Or she could be lying."

"She was very convincing when I spoke with her."

"The prosecutor may choose not to call her."

"Why wouldn't he?"

"He does not yet know that she would also testify he had been one of Constanza's visitors."

"And he will learn of this?"

"Not until just before the trial. It might put Luisa at risk for him to be aware of her knowledge. Men can be so stupid. Their brains shrink in proportion to the expansion of their penises. They think they become invisible to all but the woman they are pursuing when, in fact, eventually the world knows."

Jael laughed. "Well, there are times when a man turns a woman's brain to mush."

"I suppose. It's been a while for me."

"Beware of Dr. Micah Rand."

Danna blushed and changed the subject. "You will find Carly at Eve's Garden. It's a bordello two blocks south of the Plaza. It's not associated with a saloon. It is a rather high-class establishment patronized by the more affluent males of the vicinity. The madam is Eve. Her first name fits nicely with the business image."

"She owns the business then?"

"I'm not certain. Rumor is there is a silent partner . . . someone connected with the government. She opened the bordello about five years ago, I am told. She evidently had no shortage of capital because the building was newly constructed and included a dozen or more bed chambers."

"They do that much business?"

"I cannot personally confirm it, but I gather there is a healthy demand for this type of service."

"This may be an interesting visit. I will visit Eve's Garden first thing in the morning."

"I would wait until early afternoon. I suspect Carly works most of the night and may not get around early in the morning."

35

JAEL APPROACHED EVE'S Garden, noting that the two-floor adobe structure was set off some distance from other buildings on the block, as if no one wanted to share a common wall with the building. The building was constructed with clean, straight lines and not designed to attract undue attention. A simple, painted sign declaring that this was "Eve's Garden" was attached to the wall above the thick, oak door of the entryway.

Jael's stomach fluttered before she clasped the door handle and slowly pulled the heavy door open. She stepped into a spacious parlor furnished with stuffed settees and chairs. The walls were adorned with nude portraits of women in various seductive poses. Most of the subjects were Mexican women, but several Negresses and a token red-haired white woman were included. The sole occupant was a woman shrouded in a deep-blue velvet robe that nearly matched the color of her sapphire eyes. Jael guessed the blonde woman's age at late twenties. Even without make-up, she had a flawless complexion and was strikingly attractive. Her eyes had been fixed appraisingly on Jael since she entered the room.

Meeting the woman's gaze, Jael walked directly toward her. "I'm Jael Rivers," she said. "I'm looking for Carly."

The woman remained seated, her eyes meeting Jael's challengingly. "Carly does not service women. You would need to see Suzette for that. She's not particular."

So much for congeniality. There would be no budding friendship with this bitch. "May I speak with Eve Cambridge? It is my understanding she manages this establishment."

"I am Eve Cambridge. Make it quick."

Jael was taken aback for a moment. She was not facing her stereotypical image of a whorehouse madam. Since she was not invited to sit, Jael decided to claim a chair at a coffee table across from the Madam. "Very well. I am with the Rivers and Sinclair law firm, and I wish to speak with Carly. I understand she lives here."

"I know who you are and who you work for. You're the one who used to hump with Comanches. You are no better than anyone here."

Jael said, "I am not claiming to be better than anyone. I just wish to speak with Carly."

"What's your business with Carly?"

"It is a private matter."

"Carly is no longer with us."

"Where is she?"

"She disappeared in the middle of the night three or four days ago. Just packed up her stuff and took off without a word. Left one customer snoozing in her bed and another waiting down here. Didn't even leave my cut of the take."

"You have no idea where she went?"

"Or where she came from. I doubt if her real name was Carly. We don't ask questions. The women who show up here got to clean up good and know how to please a man. A few unhappy customers and they're out of here on their pretty asses."

"And did Carly have happy customers?"

"Not that it's any of your concern, but she was here for three years. That speaks for itself. It's a long stay in this business."

Jael caught a glimpse of movement of the curtain covering a wide opening at the end of the parlor, presumably the entrance that led to the prostitutes' cribs. Someone was listening to the conversation. Her fingers inched to the opening of her purse where her Colt was nestled. She hoped another interview was not going to end in violence.

"Did Carly have any friends here who might have an idea where she went?"

"She had no friends. The others were jealous of her clientele."

"She had elite customers?"

"Yes. She was very popular among the patrons, if you must know. But she was a snob. She didn't even speak to the other girls, other than to say *si* or no. Sometimes, *gracias* or *por favor*. I don't speak much Spanish, so I rarely got more than a broken English sentence out of her. But she talked the only language that mattered with her clients." She paused. "I've said all I'm going to say. Now, get out of here and leave me alone, or I'll call for some help that will throw you out on the street."

Jael got up to leave, keeping an eye on the curtain. Then, someone pulled it back, and a petite, stunning woman, carrying a single carpet bag, stepped out. Jael tagged her as Mexican because of the sable, shiny mane that flowed over her shoulders like a waterfall and the dark brown eyes that accentuated a light coppery-colored skin. "I am Carly. I will go with you."

This brought the Madam to her feet, her face beet-red with anger and, likely, some embarrassment at having been caught in a lie, Jael figured. "You stay right where you are, you little bitch," Eve Cambridge shrieked. "We have business to settle." She screamed, "Rufus. Come running. Problem."

Jael's fingers were on her Colt, and she had the pistol in firing position in an instant. With a nod of her head she signaled Carly to head for the door. The youthful Madam stared at the weapon, her wide eyes displaying utter disbelief. "I know how to use this. And if anyone so much as touches this young woman, I'll place a bullet between your pretty eyes," Jael snapped.

A tall, bulky man with a handle-bar moustache broke through the curtain. He wore a waist-coat and string tie, but his flinty eyes and an angry scar from the bridge of his nose to his ear made him seem out of place in this attire. Carly had already reached the outer door, and the man looked questioningly at Eve Cambridge.

"Never mind, Rufus," the Madam said softly, seeming to regain her composure some. "Let them go. We'll talk after they're gone." Her eyes locked on Carly. "My advice to you is to shut up and get out of town."

Outside, on the boardwalk, Jael spoke to Carly, who seemed very young to have spent three years as a prostitute. She did not appear to be more than twenty years of age. "You were leaving?"

"Yes. They were planning to kill me."

Jael noted that the young woman spoke without accent. "Why would they kill you?"

"Because of things I have heard and seen. They would be even more alarmed if they were aware I speak English. They assumed I was just a dumb Mexican."

"And you encouraged them to think that?"

"It has been useful in my business. The Anglos like Mexican whores and many are intimidated by a Mexican woman who speaks their language fluently. And I learn much by letting them think I do not speak English. They think I have no ears when they talk to others. I speak very little Spanish, for that matter."

They stepped onto the dusty street and strolled toward the Plaza. "But you are of Mexican descent?"

"Yes, of course. My parents lived in El Paso and worked for wealthy Anglos, and I grew up playing with their employers' children. When my father died, my mother married an Anglo, who was very kind to me and saw to my education. Then my body changed and my breasts blossomed. He started creeping into my room at night and forced me to do things I did not want to do. I ran away.

Ironic, is it not? That I ended up making my living doing the very things I tried to escape from?"

"Most of us travel trails littered with ironies." Jael hesitated. "You were obviously preparing to leave when I arrived at Eve's."

"Yes, you probably saved Eve Cambridge's life."

"What do you mean?"

"She would have refused to let me leave. I have been a virtual prisoner in the Garden since Constanza Hidalgo Robinson's death. Eve's business partners were determining what to do with me and had instructed Eve and Rufus to forbid me from leaving until they decided. I would have killed her. I carry a stiletto." She patted a little rise at the hip of her skirt, where the weapon was evidently secreted. "I certainly preferred not to kill her, but I was prepared to do so. I have used the stiletto before with troublesome clients. Surprise gets credit for most of its success."

Carly's revelation did not shock Jael in the least. She had spent much of her life in an environment where skill with a weapon was essential for survival. "Where were you planning to go?"

"First to the bank to withdraw my funds. I have set aside a tidy sum for the day I can get out of the whoring business. Then, I hoped to obtain stage passage to Denver. I doubt if that's prudent now. They will be looking for me."

"Do you have information that might harm someone?"

"I have no idea. Eve and her partners seem to think so. But I don't know what information I have that matters to anyone."

"I am working with a law firm that is representing Judge Robinson. I also have family members who have been harmed by persons connected to the judge. Would you be willing to come with me to our office to discuss what you know?"

"I need to get my money and find a way out of town."

"You said they would be looking for you. I do not think you are going to hide very easily. You are a striking young woman who will not blend in with the populace very easily. If you will talk with me, you may stay with me until it is safe for you to leave. I should warn you that my son and I may also be targets, but we are temporarily living with Danna Sinclair of our firm, and our numbers should offer some protection."

"I guess it cannot do any harm to talk. For now, I need a place to think. I will go with you to your office."

36

JAEL AND CARLY sat in the Rivers and Sinclair conference room, each nursing cups filled with steaming black coffee. Carly was a tough little bird, Jael had decided. Or she ran a good bluff. Either way, she seemed calm and relatively undaunted by her predicament.

"Carly . . . is that how you want to be called?" Jael asked.

"Yes. I've gone by Carly ever since I left home five years ago, when I was fifteen. My given name is Carmencita Reyes. I use that name for my banking."

"First, I would like to talk about the night Mrs. Robinson was killed. Do you remember that night?"

"Oh, yes. I was sent to the judge's hotel room that night."

"And this was not the first time?"

"No. For some reason I was his favorite. I generally met him weekly for at least a year. He never used anyone else . . . at the Garden anyway. Eve thought he liked Mexican women, since he was married to one."

"I am told that Constanza was very beautiful. Did you find it strange he sought comfort elsewhere?"

"No. There are men like that. They cannot perform with their wives, but they have no difficulty with prostitutes."

"And he told you he had problems performing with his wife?"

"He didn't know that I understood. But, yes, he frequently had one-sided conversations with me. He would confide his troubles . . . I guess just for the relief of telling someone else, even though he thought I did not understand English. I never told anyone about things he said. Just sort of a personal code of silence between me and my client. But now that my life could be at stake, I guess all bets are off."

"So, you were under the impression he was not having conjugal relations with his wife?"

"If you mean sex, no. I don't think he ever did have much sex with his wife. He said she ridiculed him once when he could not rise to the occasion, you might say. And I gather that pretty much killed it for him after that.

And he talked about her lovers. He sometimes cried about that while he suckled at my breast. Sorry, that's one of the things we let men do if it suits them."

"Did he ever mention the names of the lovers?"

"I didn't notice most of them. At those times, he was mostly blubbering and whining. The only one I recognized and remember was Juan Castillo. I remembered because he was an occasional client of mine. He always tipped me generously with money I did not report to the blonde witch. And he had no quirks. Always a gentleman and such a good lover I almost forgot he was just a customer. I could not blame Constanza at all where Juan was concerned. I was surprised he ever found it necessary to pay for the services I provided. But men are very strange when it comes to such things. I could write a book."

"Let's talk about the night of Constanza's death. Were you with the judge the entire night?"

"I was in the room the entire night. But he was not."

"He left the room?"

"Yes, early in the evening. He thought I was sleeping. I wasn't. I pretended to sleep because he was so distraught about something, and I wanted to spare him the frustration of failure. He has a very temperamental root, and, if he was upset or on edge, he often could not bring it to attention. But, more often than not, I could help him. I knew he would be hopeless that night, though, and even after he returned, he spurned my efforts to satisfy him. He just lay awake and stared at the ceiling. He paid his fee in the morning, however, and included a nice bonus for me. He was always generous that way, no matter how things worked out."

"Can you recall about what time he left the room?"

"I would guess in the seven o'clock vicinity. I remember checking my pendant watch not too long before he slipped out the door. He was gone for no more than an hour. I did doze off some of that time and woke when I heard him come back."

"Do you know anything about his association with the League?"

She gave Jael a quizzical look. "The League? Half of my clients are members of the League, including Andrew. That's what the judge wanted me to call him. Andrew. Except for when we were making love." She shrugged. "Then he wanted me to call him Andy. I don't know why, but that was very important to him. I can't imagine what the League has to do with anything."

"Can you give me the names of the clients you believed to be members of the League?"

"This makes me very uncomfortable. I consider the identity of my clients highly confidential."

"What if I told you the reason your life is at risk is because of what your former employers fear you might know about the League?"

"Do you think so?"

"I do. I can think of no other reason it was so important to Eve Cambridge to keep you from leaving."

"I know Andrew wanted to leave the membership. The past several months, he had taken to talking to himself about it. He even asked me once what he could do. But of course, I pretended not to understand."

"They threatened to harm him, if he quit. They depended upon his respectability and the ultimate protection of his court."

"I'm certain Eve's Garden is owned by members of the League. Eve owns a third of the business, I think, and is the manager. I doubt if a woman would be recognized as a member, but she is a critical link. The other partners are Simon Willard and Reverend Hiram Sibley. Willard visited my room on several occasions. He's a tall, gaunt man, always well-dressed and very clean. The women at the Garden appreciate a groomed and clean man. Frankly, most of them smell like stale cow shit. Eve always said that was money we smelled."

"What do you know about Willard?"

"He does something for the government, and he and Eve are real cozy. I'd guess he's close to fifty. Not handsome, really. Kind of craggy. But women like him. No trouble in the bedroom department, that's for sure. One night, he and Sibley paid triple to share me for the night. Sibley wanted to do some things that would hurt me, but I refused, and Willard backed me up. I liked him for that and treated him special. He never came to me after that night, though. I think Eve was jealous and claimed him as her exclusive. I don't think it was money between them. More like power."

"The night the two men were with you . . . did they talk business?"

"Not a lot, but while they recuperated, you might say, they talked enough that I sort of understood what they did."

"And what was that?"

"Well, Willard obviously buys stuff for the government, and Sibley helps him find sellers. Seems to be mostly cattle and horses. I think Sibley sells at high prices and Willard gets some money back for it. Doesn't sound quite legal. Maybe that's why they want the judge's backing. Anyway, it's fair to say those two run the League. I don't think there's an official members' list. Some folks just market their merchandise through Sibley because they can get the best price that way."

"From what you said, I gather you have other League members as clients."

"Well, I can't say for certain who was an actual member or who was just a seller, or how it all fits together. But, yes, I could name some ranchers and several merchants who appear to be very close to Willard and Sibley. Willard often met Sibley at the Garden, but Willard never personally met with anyone else here. It seemed to me Sibley was his go between on everything. I heard Eve tell one rancher how to find Sibley's church."

"Was Reginald Swayne one of your clients?"

"The prosecutor? During my first year, he was a regular. At least once a week. And he would pay to have me for himself the whole night. Or, if not that, he would pay extra to be first for the evening. To be honest, I don't think he liked the idea of dipping his wick where somebody else had just been."

Jael had to swallow a laugh at the young prostitute's bluntness. "Do you think Swayne was a member of the League?"

"I'd say he was close to the League. Maybe he did some legal things for them. After he left my room, I could hear his voice from downstairs talking to Eve . . . sometimes for an hour or more. I couldn't tell what they were talking about, but I guarantee he wouldn't have been up to more fornicating after leaving me."

Jael said, "We'll talk some more later. I'll take you to Danna's house with me as soon as I tend to some other things here at the office. I'm going to have Linda bring you some paper and a pencil. Perhaps you can write down the names of anyone you can think of who might have a League connection. See if you can remember anything else that might help. I don't think you are safe until we bring down the League."

Carly seemed unfazed by any danger to her life, Jael thought. She thought most of what she elicited from the prostitute was true, but she was also convinced much had been left unspoken.

37

AURELIE DID NOT return. Levi supposed she had gotten in the last word and was done with him now. He'd melted snow in his boot repeatedly, capturing a few ounces of water with each effort and quickly drinking it down until he finally had his fill. Then he placed the boot near the fire until the soaked inner sole dried to mere dampness, before he worked it back onto his foot.

He fell back into his crude nest and fell asleep again. A few hours later, he awakened. His head throbbed and bolts of pain hammered his temple. His fingers traced the flesh about the wound, and he found the swelling had ballooned. He pulled back his hand and examined and smelled the sticky substance that was oozing from the wound and confirmed his suspicion that pus was draining from the injury. He dragged himself up and sat there for some minutes, his back resting against the side of the arroyo while he took stock of his situation.

It would be a bit past sunrise now, if a man could make out the sun through the clouds and the snow that was still floating down. It did seem the snowfall was slowing some, and it appeared a good foot of the stuff had already dropped. But now a stiff wind seemed to be building up. He had some protection from the wind blasts here, but snow was starting to sweep over the edges of the ravine and could bury him before the day was out if it kept up. He leaned over and tossed the last of the wood on the fire and noted that he had used up all the fuel within easy reach. Somehow, he would have to get out and forage for more. The heat tossed off by the dancing flames was all that allowed him to cling to life. All he could do was hang on and hope. He supposed if he were a praying man, this was a time to pray. But it didn't seem right somehow that a man who had ignored the Almighty most of his life should call for help when things got a little tough. That wasn't Levi's way. Wherever he was headed, he would make the trip alone.

Firewood. That had to be his first focus. He rolled over and pressed his hands against the stone wall of the arroyo and pushed himself upright. He turned, trying to shake off the vertigo that disoriented him. He took a tentative step. And then he took another, before the black curtain dropped over his eyes again, and he toppled over onto his back, missing the fire's biting blaze by just inches. He lay on the rocky floor of the arroyo, motionless, as wind gusts began to lay a blanket of white over his still form.

38

WOLF FOUND THE tracks along the banks of
Big Goat Creek easy to follow. Nate and his
son, Eli, were obviously following the clear
creek's snaking journey into the foothills, where it ultimately cut into the Duvall land. Tabitha reined in beside
him, her dark eyes peering out of a bulky sheepskin coat
like a turtle's, he thought. Albeit a beautiful turtle.

"Why are you poking along like this?" she asked. "We
know where Pop was headed, and Nate's obviously figured that out."

"I want to be sure your dad didn't cut off somewhere
else. And we're moving at a steady pace that won't wear
down the horses. Your brother was being patient as well.
Did you see where they camped overnight a few miles
back?"

"I hadn't noticed."

"No fire. They just stopped and stretched out their bedrolls for a spell. They can't be more than three or four hours ahead of us. Probably nearing the foothills by now. I hope we can catch up to them there."

"Then we'd better keep moving." She pressed her stout bay mare out ahead of him.

Tabitha Rivers was a woman of many virtues, Wolf thought. But patience had been omitted from the list. He kneed his big gray gelding forward, but with the two spare horses packing supplies strung behind him, Wolf had no intention of trying to catch up. She would be waiting somewhere up the trail to spur him on when they met up. And he would obey if it suited him. He rarely argued with Tabitha about anything. He loved her dearly, but he had quickly learned the skill of selective hearing, and he had more than enough patience to make up for her lack of it.

It did surprise him, however, when he did not see Tabitha again until he reached the foothills a bit less than three hours later. By that time, she was sitting with a tall, rangy man and a string bean boy, who were obviously her brother and nephew, on some rocks clustered at the base of the hills. Wolf dismounted, and the man got up and strode toward him with hand extended. Wolf accepted his firm grip.

"Oliver," the man said, speaking in a voice that hinted of a Texas twang, "I'm Nate, and this is my eldest, Eli." The boy, who had remained with Tabitha, waved a friendly greeting.

"Pleasure to meet you, but I'm sorry about the circumstances."

"We appreciate your help. Tabby said you used to scout for Mackenzie when she was reporting for the *New Mexican*. I guess you're pretty well acquainted."

Wolf tossed a glance at Tabitha, who lifted her eyebrows and smiled wickedly. She had evidently left her eldest brother clueless about their relationship. "Yes," Wolf replied, "we're pretty well acquainted. What can I do to help out?"

It was late afternoon, and the ground here was blanketed by several inches of snow. Cloud cover nearly obscured the mountain peaks, and Wolf didn't like the feel of the wind that was picking up. None of this portended well for any search for Levi Rivers or his body. It occurred to him they might be picking up the search again next spring, but he was not about to suggest this possibility to Tabitha Rivers or her brother.

Nate said, "I think Eli came across a place where Pop camped. It's further up the slope some distance, near some scrub trees. Want to take a look?"

"Yes, I'd like that. Let me stake out my horses, and then you can show me."

Tabitha leaped up from the flat-topped boulder she had been sitting on. "I can help with that."

"Why, thank you, Miss Rivers. I hate to impose upon a mere acquaintance for such menial labor," Wolf replied.

Tabitha took the reins of one of the spare horses. Nate Rivers watched with a confused expression on his face. Shortly, Nate led the parties on foot a quarter mile over rough terrain uphill to the suspected campsite. When they reached the spot, he pointed to the charred wood and dead coals that remained from the campfire.

"Not the best site," Nate observed. "High ground. Rough. Only these scrub trees and brush for protection. Not near the water."

"It's a good view of anything coming from three directions. I wonder if somebody was following him and he picked up on it?"

"If that was the case, why would you build a fire that could be seen for miles. It's like an invitation."

"Maybe it was," Wolf said.

"He wanted to draw somebody up here?"

"Just a possibility. He could have burrowed in behind the clump of trees and brush and waited. Regardless, he had a good view from here, so it would be hard for a man to sneak up on him."

Nate said, "His horse was saddled when it came back, so it doesn't seem likely he was ambushed here. Besides, Eli and I have spent three or four hours searching every inch of this section of the hills. No sign of Pop."

"Where are we from the Duvall land?"

"We're still on Slash R ground here. Duvall's starts about a mile due west. The creek leads you right into the middle of it. There's a narrow cut through the mountains that opens up on a wide valley with prime grazing. It's virgin country as far as cattle are concerned. The place is pretty much landlocked, if you don't enter from the Slash R. Duvall's never run cows there because he'd have to bring them over mountains from the north if we didn't let him pass. Of course, we would have. It wouldn't be right to deny a man access to his own property. Pop wanted that place in the worst way, and I suppose it made him blind to anything else. I've got to admit I'd love to expand the herd and run cattle in that valley. The mountains make a natural fence on all sides, and Big Goat assures a water supply. You've got to move the herds out early, though, because there's a lot of snow up this high."

"So," Wolf said, "if he was still determined to check out the Duvall acres, which way do you think he would go?"

"Hard to say. Either he went for the valley or he rode into the mountains to overlook the whole thing. Probably two thousand acres on this north side are mountains and pine. My brother, Ham, always thought some of our forest ought to go into timber production to help with cash needs and reduce debt. This would be a natural addition to that business, and Pop had started to give in to the idea some."

Wolf had a hunch that Levi Rivers was the kind of man who would want to see as much of the land as he could. From all he had heard about Levi, the rancher was a visionary, an empire builder, and he would want to view the property from its highest point.

"I'll try to find the mountain trail," Wolf said. "Maybe the rest of you can head into the valley and spread out and see what you turn up. If anybody finds anything, start a fire and make as much smoke as you can." He didn't say so, but he expected any find to be Levi Rivers's body.

Nate chuckled. "I'll bet you were an officer in somebody's army."

"Major. First Cherokee Brigade, Confederate Army. Why do you say that?"

"You're a man who can't help taking charge."

"I apologize. I didn't mean any offense. I forget sometimes."

"No offense taken. This is too personal for Tabby and me. Our judgment might be clouded. Your idea sounds okay to me."

"Not to me," Tabitha chimed in. "I'm going with you Oliver. You're not my major."

Wolf sighed and shrugged with resignation. A fuss over this would be a waste of valuable time.

"The sky's clearing," Wolf said. "And there should be a full moon tonight. I'm going to walk. With the snow, footing will be treacherous for the horses, and I can't read signs if I'm mounted. Horses will slow us down in this terrain."

Nate said, "It'll be quite a string, but we'll take all the horses and meet you back here no later than this time tomorrow. If Pop's out here someplace, considering when that spooky gelding returned home, he's got to be within six hours away . . . under normal weather conditions. Even if he's not hurt, he couldn't have walked that far."

"If he wasn't hurt," Tabitha remarked, "we would have met him on the trail."

39

WOLF AND TABITHA reached the mountain's base in less than half an hour. Wolf had anchored the lighter supplies, including snowshoes and several lariats, to Tabitha's back. He carried the filled canteens, a few food supplies, an axe, and a rolled-up buffalo robe, along with Tabitha's Henry rifle. He left his Winchester in its scabbard on the gelding, since Tabitha would not let the Henry out of her sight. She had recovered it from a Tonkawa warrior Jael had killed with her bow and a well-placed arrow. It was a fine weapon, not readily available, and she always knew its whereabouts, Wolf had learned. He also knew there was no better marksman in New Mexico Territory than Tabitha Rivers.

Wolf led the way as they moved into the high country. He quickly found a likely deer trail, revealed by telltale hoof prints in the snow. A narrow path twisting through brush and tree limbs had been carved out by frequent travel, and it ran parallel to, and no more than twenty feet distant from, the rim that overlooked the valley. The full moon lit up the snow-blanketed earth below, and when they broke through the brush on one occasion and stepped to the rim's edge, they could see Nate and Eli with their string of horses moving like ants across the valley floor.

When they returned to the trail, Wolf's eye caught sight of something fluttering on the brambles of a gooseberry bush. He tugged it free and showed it to Tabitha. "Horse hair. Some critter left a few strands of this tail on the barbs. Somebody rode up this trail not long ago."

"But was it Pop, or somebody who was planning to kill him?"

"Either way, it increases the odds this trail leads to your father."

The trail grew steeper and rockier as they trudged higher up the mountainside. The snow deepened as well and increasingly pulled at their feet, and the wind lashed at their faces and resisted their climb. Finally, they stopped, and Wolf removed the snowshoes from the bonds on Tabitha's back, and they strapped the implements to their feet. This lightened their feet, and they picked up the pace as they wound through the forest.

Tabitha did not once utter a complaint, Wolf noted, and she kept up with his stride with surprisingly little difficulty. Of course, she had lived with the Comanche for a year, which no doubt left her in prime physical shape.

After nearly five hours of hiking, they found themselves within a half mile of the summit. The air at this altitude left them both breathing heavier, and they leaned against some pines to catch their breaths for the final leg of the climb.

Tabitha asked, "What do you expect to find? There have been no more signs. I'm wondering if we passed him someplace."

"If we don't come across anything, we'll look around the area and then work our way back down, hoping we see something we missed. We should get a good view of the entire landscape up here. Maybe we'll pick up a sign. Tabby, you do understand that with this snow, we just might not find anything?"

"And, if we don't, it means Pop is dead, and we might not ever know what happened to him. The not knowing will make losing him even worse. I guess you've figured out that Pop and I were very close. He spoiled me rotten, yet he taught me how to survive, coached me, and pushed me to be the best at whatever I did. He complained I wasn't learning the domestic skills I needed to be a good wife, but he never let me hang around Mom enough to learn. Not that I ever objected. I always wanted to be with Pop. I couldn't get excited about the stuff Mom did. Still, she was our school teacher, and I owe her any writing skills I have. That's it. She was always more my stern school teacher than my mother. I never thought about it before. I loved her, and I value what she taught me, but there was a distance between us, like she conceded me to Pop's domain. Anyway, I lost the chance to change things the day the Comanche struck the ranch." Her voice softened. "I can't lose Pop yet. I'm not ready. And I'm to blame."

"You did what you had to do, and from what you tell me, Levi Rivers would be the first man to say it. And if you feel you must take responsibility, start forgiving yourself. If you don't, you'll end up less than you can be. Not much of a tribute to your father."

She looked at him through the fog of her breath, and he could see she was miffed at him. Good. It would spark her to keep going. He pushed away from the tree and started moving up the trail.

Wolf raised his hand, signaling Tabitha to stop, when he saw the frozen corpse sprawled face-down on the rocky table of the precipice that overlooked the valley. The ledge was nearly swept clean by the wind gusts, but a crust of snow had molded to the form of the man who lay there. Oddly, he appeared to be naked, except for his booted feet. Tabitha came up beside Wolf, following his gaze.

"No, no!" she screamed. "Pop. No." She broke past Wolf and charged toward the body as fast as the awkward gait of her snowshoes would allow. She was bent over the body, frantically scraping and brushing away the ice and snow before Wolf joined her, her gut-wrenching wailing fading into the chorus of the wind. Then, abruptly she stopped and turned silent. "This isn't Pop," she said.

Wolf got down on his knees beside her. "No. This is a young man."

"Thank God." Then she paused. "That's terrible of me to say. This is somebody's son or even some child's father."

The body was frozen to the stone, and with some effort, Wolf pried it free and rolled it over. Pale blue eyes stared at him from an ice-glazed face, like the man was surprised to be found in this condition. His bare chest was caked with frozen blood and marked clearly with two distinct bullet wounds.

"Oh, my God. It's Tobe. What's he doing up here? What happened to him?"

"You know this man?"

"Yes. He's Tobe Duvall. His uncle, Jed Duvall, owns the land that Pop was checking out. He's about my age. His father was a drunk and got killed in a gunfight when Tobe wasn't more than twelve or thirteen. A year later Jed married Tobe's mother, but Tobe didn't get along with his uncle, who became his stepfather. He was always in trouble it seemed. I would run into him at socials sometimes. I had to slap him once when he got too familiar with my breasts. He was drunk and said he was sorry. I sort of liked him, though. He could be charming when he wanted his way. He was something of a lost soul, I think."

"I suspect your father killed him."

"But why?"

"It's a fair guess this young man was involved in luring him into a trap and caught his own foot in it."

"But where's Pop?"

"That's what we've got to figure out."

Rays of sunlight were creeping over the horizon now, and Wolf removed his snowshoes and began to slowly pace the ledge and surrounding terrain. Soon he came across the caked blood spots some ten feet back from the edge of the precipice. Then he walked to the edge that dropped off into the abyss below. Stone outcroppings jutted from the face of the mountain face and there was a huge escarpment no more than one hundred fifty feet below, where a body, horse or human, should have landed before dropping another thousand feet beyond.

"You've got some thoughts," Tabitha said. "Please share them."

"I think your father was wounded here. Young Duvall wouldn't have crawled anyplace after taking those shots, and there's blood over there." He pointed to where he had discovered the residue. "The good news is I don't see any sign that your father went over the edge. Also, I don't think it's likely Duvall would have undressed himself after being shot down. That suggests your father stripped him, probably to salvage any garments for his own survival. He probably wasn't in any shape to make the trek down the slope after his horse took off. He obviously didn't capture Duvall's horse, or we would have encountered him on the trail here."

"That means he shouldn't be far from here."

"No. But this altercation must have happened several days ago, and we've had a big snow since then."

"You're telling me not to get my hopes up."

"I am."

"He's up here. And he's alive. I can feel it."

Wolf didn't remind her that minutes earlier she thought her father was dead.

"Okay, from here to the rim, you and I are going to start walking semi-circles about twenty-feet apart. We'll keep moving outward until we find something"

Wolf put his snowshoes back on, and they began their search, each surveying the land on each side of the paths they traipsed for some sign of Levi Rivers. Once a swing was completed, they would move further from their starting places and commence the walk again. Thirty minutes later, Tabitha suddenly disappeared from Wolf's sight.

"Tabby," Wolf called. "Where are you?"

"Over here," she yelled, her head popping up like a jack-in-the-box. "I walked off into a ravine. Pop's down here, but I don't know if he's alive. Hurry."

40

WOLF SLID DOWN the side of the arroyo and found Tabitha kneeling by Levi Rivers, brushing the snow from his face. The man didn't look much better than young Duvall, and Wolf feared he was dead, or, if not, soon would be.

"He's alive," Tabby said in a near whisper, unable to contain the excitement in her voice. "He's breathing. But he's near frozen, and his head looks awful. And he doesn't move. It's like he's sleeping, but he won't wake up."

Wolf slipped in beside her. He checked the man for a pulse. It wasn't Tabitha's imagination. The old rancher was alive. Barely. He took inventory of their location. Smart man. Levi had found himself a natural shelter in the arroyo under the overhanging boughs of trees. A scattering of charred wood remnants indicated he had maintained a fire for a time. That's what they needed now. He stood up and worked the rolled buffalo robe off his back.

"Tabby, let's get your father wrapped in this robe, and then I'll get a fire started. We've got to get him warmed up. Fast."

Soon they had Levi wrapped like a mummy in the buffalo robe. Wolf gathered some firewood and quickly had a healthy fire crackling and warding off the chill for the three of them. His next task was to signal the other searchers. He returned to the precipice and started another fire on the ledge. He cut pine and cedar branches from live trees and gathered the few leaves that could be found under the snow and soon had thick smoke curling toward the sky. It was mid-morning and the sky was clear. Even the wind was letting up. The gods are smiling, he thought. He would keep feeding the fire until they departed, but he was confident the smoke would be seen from the valley.

As he backed away from the smoke, Wolf nearly stumbled over Tobe Duvall's body. He supposed the boy deserved something better than the wolves and vultures and other carrion-eaters would deliver as soon as the sun started to do its work. He grabbed an ankle and dragged the corpse back to the arroyo.

Tabitha heard Wolf approaching and stood up to peer out. "What are you doing?"

"Before we leave, I'll drop him in here and cover him with stones."

"Why?"

"Why not?"

"Because he came to murder my father."

"He won't know one way or the other now, but I will."

She shrugged. "If that's what you've got to do."

"That's what I've got to do. Anything happening with your father?"

"Nothing. I guess he's in what they call a coma."

Wolf joined her in the arroyo. "Might be best until we get him off this mountain."

He knelt by Levi and took time now to examine the mass on his forehead. The swollen flesh drooped over and covered his right eye entirely. "He took a bullet in his skull."

"Can you remove it?"

"I'm not brave enough to tamper with a head wound. I might do more damage. He needs a surgeon. The swelling is from the putrefaction. I saw a lot of it during the war. I should be able to do something about that. I don't know if it will help, but I'm sure it won't do harm."

"What can you do?"

Wolf plucked his skinning knife from its sheath and handed it to Tabitha. "Heat the tip on the fire. I'll find something to clean the wound with."

The best he could come up with was a flannel shirt Levi must have taken off of Tobe Duvall. He tore some of it into strips for bandages and kept the remainder for wiping off the unpleasantness that was about to ensue. He pulled the buffalo robe away from Levi's head and turned his head to one side. "Ready for the knife," he said.

Tabitha handed Wolf the knife, and, with no hesitation, he swept the razor-sharp blade across the swollen flesh, leaving an incision about two inches in length. Immediately, brownish-yellow pus and blood began to seep from the cut. Using some of the flannel to sop up the mess, he began to press on the flesh around the opening until the pus erupted like a tiny geyser and poured out of the flesh. He was prepared for the putrid odor, or he might have gagged, and a glance at Tabitha revealed she had turned her head away. He continued to manipulate the flesh until it shrunk into a puckered sack. Levi's eye was now visible again, and the pressure on his forehead was temporarily relieved. Wolf wrapped several strips of cloth around Levi's head to staunch the bleeding. He had no idea whether the procedure helped or not, but at least the rancher's face appeared less grotesque.

"Now we've got to get him down the mountain, so we can get him to a surgeon," Wolf said.

"The nearest is Santa Fe. That's three days, if we're lucky."

"Then we'll make some luck. First, we need to make a sled."

"A sled?"

"I knew my axe would be good for something."

Wolf climbed out of the arroyo and quickly selected a pair of likely young trees. He cut them down and trimmed the branches, ending up with two long poles. He fashioned half a dozen crossbars from the branches and lashed them with rawhide strips to the poles to form a crude stretcher. When that was finished, he anchored the ends of a lariat to each of the poles to make a pull-rope. Then he pulled it to the bank of the arroyo, noting with satisfaction that it glided quite nicely over the snow. Of course, a man of Levi's size laid out on top would make a more challenging pull.

A few minutes later, Wolf lifted Levi from the robe while Tabitha snatched it up, scrambled up the slope, and rolled it out on the stretcher. Wolf, pushing his powerful arms and shoulders to the limit, carried Levi to the arroyo's bank where the stretcher waited, and with Tabitha's help eased him on to the mountain ambulance. They took the other rope and anchored Levi to the sled-stretcher. It required another fifteen minutes to drop Tobe Duvall's body in the arroyo and roll and toss in enough stones to cover him. Finally, they were ready to pull out.

"The trip down will go faster," Wolf said. "I think we can meet the others before dark. If we don't have a wagon, we'll convert our stretcher to a travois and keep moving."

"Oliver, you're leaving me breathless."

"Good. I want to keep you that way the rest of our days."

41

WOLF AND TABITHA reached the foothills with the comatose Levi Rivers several hours before sundown. Tabitha had followed the stretcher bearing her father, as Wolf, harnessing himself to the rope, raced down the mountainside. They paused only to negotiate a sharp turn in the trail or to wedge between occasional boulders that lined the trail. The Cherokee's stamina and strength constantly kept her in awe, but it was his innate intelligence that most drew her to him. Increasingly, she was beginning to see him as a man for all seasons and years of one's life. She had difficulty envisioning an existence without him as a part of it.

She looked at her father, wrapped in the robe, teetering on the edge of death. He had not met Wolf, and she was further distressed and saddened at the thought Levi

Rivers might never meet the man she had come to love. He could not die now. She simply would not permit it.

Tabitha's mood brightened when she caught sight of her eldest brother and Eli waiting with the horses at the place where they had parted so many hours ago. Then Nate's gelding lunged forward and started up the slope toward Wolf and Tabitha. In a few minutes, Nate reined in his horse and dismounted, looking first at the stretcher and then to Tabitha.

"He's alive," she said, anticipating his unasked question, and joined him at their father's side.

"Have you spoken with him?" Nate asked.

"No. He's been like this since we found him." She told him about finding Tobe Duvall's body and the scenario she and Wolf had pieced together.

"We've got to get him to Santa Fe," Nate said. "Josh is here with a buckboard. Trail's too rough and steep to get it up here. He's waiting about two miles out along the creek. He brought an extra team of mules. I'll have Eli hightail it over to let him know Pop's alive and to hitch up both teams and be ready to ride." He mounted and returned to his son, who was waiting with the horses.

When Wolf and Tabitha reached the horses, Wolf quickly and deftly bound the travois to one of the pack horses and led the horse away behind his own for the rendezvous with Josh. As they rode, Wolf spoke, "Tabby, why don't you ride in the buckboard with your dad. Josh can handle the mules and wagon. Nate can take a few of the horses and ride as lookout. Eli and I will head back to the Slash R to tell Dawn what's happened and get her and others that need to come on the trail to Santa Fe. I'll pick up Owl and Smokey, too, and bring them with me. I'll probably pass you on the trail on my way to Santa Fe. I'll let Doc Rand know you're on the way, and maybe he can ride out to meet you."

"Why can't you stay with us?"

"I've got business with the newspaper."

"Newspaper? I'm the reporter."

"And it's time your story got printed. The first of the series."

42

WOLF HAD NOT dressed in a suit and tie for some years, and the stiff collar of the white shirt chafed his neck. After a quick bath and shave at the barber's, his next stop had been at Spiegelbergs', where a young commission clerk in the men's department had been delighted to outfit him in expensive Sunday go-to-meeting attire, including the charcoal-gray suit and vest and a pair of Mexican-tooled, black cowboy boots. His next stop was the *Santa Fe Daily New Mexican*, where he was headed now. And then he would pay a call on the law firm of Rivers and Sinclair.

Wolf entered the dingy, crowded offices of the *New Mexican*. These folks could use his construction and designing services, he thought. The plaster on the walls was crumbling off in places, and the warped board ceiling was rife with spots where rainwater had invaded. A young woman and three older men were bent over type-writers at ancient desks in a single, open room, separated from him by a deeply pocked and scratched cedarwood counter. There appeared to be three small private offices along one wall, and the click-clack sound from the rear of the building indicated that the pressroom was housed there.

He stood at the counter several minutes before he was noticed by the young woman, who he guessed would be no more than nineteen or twenty years old. She had chestnut-colored hair and was quite pretty, and he thought that if he were unattached he might like to know her better. She came to the counter, her azure eyes appraising him unashamedly. He did not mind.

"I'm Harriet," she said. "May I help you?"

"Yes. My name's Oliver Wolf. I would like to see your publisher, Ansel Jackman, about an important business matter." He was quite certain Jackman was still out of the Territory.

"I'm sorry. Mr. Jackman is out of town. He isn't expected back in the office for several weeks. Could someone else be of assistance?"

"I was told that a Mr. Thorne might be helpful. Is he available?"

"That would be Edmund Thorne. He's the news editor. Mr. Jackman acts as publisher and editor-in-chief. Ed's sort of his second in command, you might say. I'll check with him and see if he's available to see you." She whisked away and walked briskly to the furthest office while Wolf's eyes followed the bounce of her nice bottom.

He could hear the murmur of a conversation coming through the open office door, and a male's whiney voice suggested Thorne did not wish to be bothered. Harriet seemed to be pleading Wolf's case, however. Soon, Harriet returned with a mischievous smile on her face. "He's very busy. But he decided he would make time for you. He will be out shortly. Please be seated."

"Thank you, Harriet. I truly appreciate your help."

She paused a moment, evidently waiting for him to say something else, before she said, "You are welcome," and returned to her desk.

Wolf sat down in what appeared to be the more solid of two straight-back chairs in the narrow waiting space. He was a patient man, but his patience was wearing thin when a thirtyish, horse-faced man appeared a half hour later.

"Mr. Wolf," the man said, coming around the counter and extending his hand, "I am Edmund Thorne. Miss Gerber says you have important business to discuss."

Wolf accepted a grip limp as a wet noodle and applied enough pressure of his own to make the news editor flinch. "My pleasure. I believe you will want to hear what I have to say."

"Very well. Follow me." Thorne led Wolf toward his office, and as Wolf passed Harriet's desk, she shrugged and gave an empty-handed gesture as if apologizing for his wait. He instinctively liked Harriet. She was one of those persons that kept a business running despite sloppy management. He guessed that she watched the publisher's back, and Thorne probably knew it.

Thorne's office was so small the news editor had to squeeze between the wall and his desktop to get behind it. He gestured for Wolf to take the single chair in front of the desk.

"Now, Mr. Wolf, I have deadlines to meet. Would you mind stating your business?"

"Of course, I'm considering establishing a newspaper in competition with the *New Mexican*."

Thorne's face flushed, and he was silent for several moments. "I see. And what does this have to do with me?"

"You will have to explain to your publisher why your neglect of an important story caused him to have serious competition in the Territory's newspaper business."

"What story?"

"I have been offered a story by Tabitha Rivers. You are acquainted with her?"

Thorne glared at Wolfe and his mouth twisted before he spoke. "Of course. She's a reporter here."

"She also has freelance status and is quite famous, I understand."

"Famous might be an overstatement, but she has a following."

"I think your publisher might say your newspaper needs her more than she needs the newspaper."

"What's this about?"

"Miss Rivers submitted a story to you about an organization sometimes referred to as the League. It told of her beating and threats that were made against her family as a result of her investigation of the League. You refused to publish it. I informed her I would do so, and I intend to go from here to a local printer to arrange for the first single-story issue of the *Santa Fe Courier*. We will start small, but I am not accustomed to failure. The Rivers family will back me in this endeavor. Tabitha Rivers will be managing editor and will continue her series on the League members and their enterprises."

All color had drained from Thorne's face, and his fingers tapped nervously on his desktop. "Santa Fe cannot support two newspapers."

"Yes, I suppose not. Well, the *New Mexican* has had a nice run."

"You didn't come here just to inform me of your new publication."

"You're very insightful, Edmund. May I call you Edmund?"

Thorne did not reply to Wolf's question. "Tell me what you have in mind."

"If you publish Miss Rivers's story in tomorrow's issue and thereafter continue her series on the League, the *Courier* will not be born."

Thorne was sweating profusely now. "You don't understand. You see, I have been threatened also."

"By whom?"

"I can't say."

"The stories are going to be published. And when they are, the League's fangs will be removed one at a time until it is virtually toothless. Others are starting to recognize this. Have you ever considered that your courage to forge ahead might make give you some personal recognition? A raise? A pathway to a better position? Edmund Thorne: crusader for justice."

"The man who delivered the threat was the Territorial Attorney, Reginald Swayne. He was the messenger for the League."

"Having disclosed that, will you publish the story?"

"Front page. Tomorrow's issue. The next day, I will publish an editorial that recites Swayne's threats."

"The *Courier* just died, Edmund."

43

UPON WOLF'S ARRIVAL at the office, Danna summoned Marty Locke and Jael to join her in the conference room. Wolf was sitting at the table and stood when Jael entered. Jael smiled, put her hands on her hips and cocked her head to one side as she looked him over. "I didn't recognize you at first, Oliver. Is there a funeral I should know about?"

Danna thought Wolf was an imposing presence in his ordinary appearance, but his business attire had transformed him into an even more formidable figure, a man of authority to be taken seriously.

Pulling back a chair for Jael, Wolf said, "Yes. I'm preparing a funeral for the League."

After they were all seated, Jael asked, "Do you have any word about Levi?"

Wolf gave his friends an abbreviated version of the finding and recovery of Levi Rivers. "Josh and Tabby are bringing Levi to Santa Fe in a buckboard. Right now, I would guess they are about four hours out. I went directly to Dr. Rand when I arrived, and then I visited the marshal's office. Marshal Calder was going to accompany the surgeon to meet up with the wagon. Levi has regained consciousness but is delirious . . . keeps having quarrels with his late wife. Tabby thinks they're arguing about her, but she can't tell what it's all about. At least, during his periods of consciousness, she has been able to get him to take water. That's critical. The entire Rivers family will be gathering here in Santa Fe, I'm sure. And after tomorrow morning, I don't think their lives will be in danger."

"Why do you say that?" Danna asked.

"I had a discussion with Mr. Thorne at the *New Mexican*. Tabby's story about the League will be printed tomorrow. I don't think anyone in the League will be initiating violence against the family after that."

Wolf's remarks made Danna uneasy. "Thorne hasn't suffered any injuries, I assume."

Wolf shot her a look of incredulity, which she was certain was feigned. "Why would you think that? No, he is fine, if you don't consider bruises to his ego. Now, I am going to visit the good Reverend Hiram Sibley, but I thought I might see if we could share some information first."

"What kind of information?" Danna asked.

"I would like to see if, together, we can untangle the structure of this League. I know you are defending Judge Robinson against charges of murdering his wife, which may or may not be related."

Marty Locke spoke. "I can't reveal any of my conversations with Judge Robinson, but other information can be shared in general terms, if it might be helpful to his defense. If crimes are involved, we may even have an obligation to make proper officials aware of some things we have learned. Of course, you have no official status."

"No, I do not."

Danna said, "Jael has spoken with important witnesses. I'm not comfortable disclosing their names, but I think she could share her thoughts on the structure of the League and how it works. Jael, why don't you do that? I'll interrupt if I decide we are getting into confidentiality issues."

Jael said. "I don't think any of this is very complicated. The purpose of the League is to take advantage of the stupidity of bureaucrats who manage the distribution of funds for purchasing military supplies and allotments for the reservations. I have a particular interest because of the firm's representation of the Comanche at the Fort Sill Reservation . . . Quanah specifically."

"And how do they take advantage?"

"It's a system of kickbacks at every level. Simon Willard, the General Procurement Officer, receives a budget for purchasing horses, cattle and food supplies for the Army. He may have another budget for buying cattle, food and clothing for the reservations. Reverend Sibley employs people to deal with merchants and ranchers to provide the products. The sellers get paid top prices for selling through Sibley, and sign receipts for fifteen percent more than they actually get paid. Sibley and Willard split the fifteen percent. Sibley probably pays the workers out of his share. The percentages are just conjecture. I must confess that our ward, Rylee O'Brian, outlined how this would work. As you know, she assists Willi Spiegelberg at the Second National and is learning accounting procedures at the Spiegelberg merchandising enterprises as well."

"The Spiegelbergs are not a part of the League then?"

"No. They probably wouldn't let Jews in." She smiled. "That would exclude Comanche Jews, too, so I'd be out. Honestly, I don't think the Spiegelbergs would have anything to do with it anyway. But they may know something's been going on. Rylee says they aren't given an opportunity to bid on government contracts."

"The procurement agent would have budgets into the hundreds of thousands of dollars," Wolf said. "This could be very lucrative for the participants."

Danna remarked, "That's why they need a prosecutor and a judge who will be blind and deaf to any complaints. There are a good many honest ranchers and merchants out there who would have nothing to do with the schemes and might report what's going on. From time to time one of these folks is beaten or ends up dead to keep everyone else quiet. The League's threats are taken seriously."

"For what it's worth," Jael said, "Eve Cambridge, the madam at Eve's Garden, appears to be an important intermediary between Sibley and Willard. I haven't nailed down just how dispensable she is to the operation, but I have a cooperative witness."

Marty said, "Willard seems to have insulated himself with multiple layers of deniability. Tabitha's stories will probably bring down the League, but they won't be enough to put the leaders in jail. That's not my concern, though. Danna and I have a client to defend. Oliver, do you have any information that will help us defend Judge Robinson?"

"No. I promised previously I will share any information I obtain with you, and will do so. He seems to have set himself up as the logical suspect. I barely know the man. Do you think he's that stupid? Or did he purposely set himself up?"

"Why would he do that?" Marty asked.

"That's the question, isn't it? Now, I appreciate your thoughts. You've been very helpful. But I have selfish objectives here. I want Tabby to write and publish her League series, and I intend to assure she doesn't get killed in the process. Now, I'm going to pursue those goals with a visit to Reverend Sibley."

"And I am going with you," Danna said. "I've met this snake, and I think another gun and witness would be good insurance. Besides, he might let something slip that would be useful to our case. We can rent a buggy. You may continue your role as a prospective newspaper publisher. I'll be your lawyer."

Wolf's silence made her wonder if he was going to buy in to her idea. Finally, he nodded his head affirmatively and got up. "I'll rent the buggy and be back in a half hour," he said.

44

WOLF HAD NOTICED at least two sentries posted in the hills a half-mile or more beyond the church compound, so he figured someone must have signaled their approach. He pulled the buggy to a halt in front of the church building. Sibley stood with crossed arms on the top step that led to the entryway to the church. Two men, obviously hired guns, hovered nearby, one on each side of him, a dozen feet away from their boss.

"Stay put," Wolf instructed Danna softly. "I'll see if I can wangle an invitation to sit down someplace and chat."

Wolf stepped down from the buggy, brushing the Army Colt in the holster beneath his jacket with the tips of his fingers, to confirm its readiness. He had not expected to be met with such open hostility, and he worried he had put Danna's life in danger. Sibley watched him with squinted eyes as he approached.

"Reverend Sibley," he said. "My name's Oliver Wolf."

"I know who the hell you are. And I saw what you did to Lash. Those fancy duds don't change the fact you're nothing but a breed trying to pretend he's a white man."

The man's words did not rise to the level of a gnat bite to Wolf. He had long ago steeled himself to the opinions of men like Sibley. Wolf valued all men by what they could do and produce. And that included himself. "Reverend Sibley, I am considering establishment of a newspaper in Santa Fe, and I understand you have funds for investment in new enterprises."

"Go to hell," Sibley snapped. "I've heard about your newspaper business and the deal you forced on the *New Mexican*."

Edmund Thorne had not wasted any time getting word to Sibley. Further evidence that the so-called preacher carried out foreman duties for the League. "All right, Sibley, no more games. This is how it's going to work. The stories will start in the *New Mexican* tomorrow. If they don't, the *Courier* will be in print the next day. Your name will be in the following day's story. Don't look for protection from the prosecutor on your payroll. He's likely to be one of the defendants. A special prosecutor from out of the territory will be here within a month to handle the cases. But if I were you, I'd be more worried about the Rivers family. They're gathering in Santa Fe, and you're going to have a target on your forehead. I wish you luck in making it to a courtroom."

Sibley gave a barely perceptible nod, and a gun's sharp crack stung Wolf's ears. Wolf saw the gunman to Sibley's left stumble backward before a second shot was fired and took him down. Wolf had his Colt in his hand and placed a shot in the second gunslinger's belly before the man could squeeze the trigger of the pistol aimed at Danna. Then he wheeled and pointed the Colt at Sibley, who already had his hands raised.

"I'm not armed," Sibley screamed. "I'm not armed."

Danna climbed out of the buggy, her six-gun still in her hand, and hurried up the steps toward Sibley. She pointed the weapon at his head. "Unbuckle your belt and drop your trousers."

The man paled. "What are you doing? You're insane."

Wolf looked on with curiosity. "I'd do it if I were you, Preacher."

Sibley complied. Danna pushed her free hand down the terrified man's undershorts, grasped something and yanked sharply. Sibley squealed.

Danna turned away and spoke to Wolf. "Let me have that clean handkerchief in your coat pocket." Wolf removed the white handkerchief and handed it to Danna, who carefully placed five or six pubic hairs on it, and folded it over.

45

D R. MICAH RAND took command after Josh and Nate Rivers helped him maneuver Wolf's stretcher into the surgery and carefully lifted Levi onto the table. Levi was a tall man, and his feet hung over the table's edge. The white-painted table had once seen service in someone's kitchen and now served as his examination and surgery table. As a former Army surgeon, Rand had worked in much more primitive facilities.

"I need one person to assist me with surgery. I will have to ask everyone else to leave, and I hope you will keep others away until we're finished."

"I'm your assistant," Tabitha said. She saw her brothers were going to protest. But she gave them what her siblings always called "Tabby's glare" and they backed off.

"If you change your mind, Sis, we'll be right outside the door," Josh said.

After her brothers left the surgery, Tabitha removed her thick coat and tossed it on a chair. "What do you want me to do, Doctor?"

"Just hold your father's hand while I examine him. He's unconscious now, but I don't know how deeply he's out. I have chloroform, but I would prefer not to use the stuff. It can be tricky and risky. Frankly, I don't see any reason your father should be alive after what he's been through."

"He's tougher than a boot. Pop's going to make it through this."

"If he does, he can thank you and Oliver Wolf. That incision to drain the wound bought some serious time. Between the putrefaction and the pressure on his brain, he would have been dead by now."

"That was Oliver's idea."

"Well, we haven't seen the end of those problems, but our immediate concern is to remove the bullet. I'm going to do some probing without anesthetic and see how we get along."

Tabitha clutched Levi's hand and watched Rand's deft fingers do their work. He spent a lot of time cleansing the entry wound with water and wiping an orange-colored liquid on the flesh surrounding the wound.

"Iodine," he said, evidently sensing her curiosity. "Some doctors are suggesting there are unseen microorganisms that cause infections and kill the patient as often as the injury. Old fashioned cleanliness seems to be the newest innovation in medicine. Makes sense to me."

He placed some stitches in the incision Wolf had made and pointed out, "I'm leaving a gap at one end, so we can continue drainage at this point. I have a tiny tube I'll insert later. I'll do the same at the entry wound."

Finally, he opened a glass case next to the table, spread out a clean cloth on top and removed some instruments and placed them on the cloth. He selected a probe and inched it carefully into the wound. "Eureka," he exclaimed, after just a few minutes. "Found it. Not too deeply imbedded in bone."

Rand plucked a pair of forceps from his instrument line-up and worked the narrow nose into the wound.

Tabitha watched his fingers tighten, as the instrument seemed to grasp something. The surgeon gave a gentle tug, and removed the slug, which was trailed by a rivulet of scarlet blood. "We'll let it drain a bit before we staunch the bleeding."

He removed some more white cloths from a shelf and tucked several beneath Levi's head to catch the blood. "I'm glad the anesthesia wasn't necessary, but I would have preferred some reaction. He's in a state of absolute unconsciousness." He grabbed a wrist and checked the patient's pulse. "Quite strong and steady. I'll check it every fifteen minutes or so. A serious slowing might indicate internal hemorrhage inside the skull. Frankly, this is a lot of guesswork, and there is not a lot we can do but wait. I have two patient rooms here. Why don't you call your brothers in to help us move him to a bed?"

46

"I HAVE A specimen for you," Danna said, presenting Dr. Micah Rand with the folded handkerchief she had confiscated from Wolf. "Open it carefully."

Rand unfolded the satiny cloth and examined the contents. He gave Danna a mildly exasperated look. "Has anyone suggested that the women in your office gather strange collections?"

"These aren't collections. We're gathering potential evidence."

"I don't even want to know how you came up with these or who you took them from."

"That's quite all right. I just want to know if we have a match. I'm not expecting one, but I had an opportunity."

"If you want to come with me, I can check it out now. I'm waiting for the Rivers family to leave Levi's room. I gave them another twenty minutes."

Danna followed Rand into the examination-surgery-laboratory room. "Jael told me you removed the bullet and that Levi had come around a time or two."

"Yes. You might say he's semi-conscious. He's taken water and even a little chicken broth when he's awake. That's most important right now. Water and some nourishment. He doesn't talk much sense when he's conscious, but any reaction is progress."

Danna recalled that Jael had said Levi kept rambling on about Aurelie, his late wife. Jael feared, at first, that Dawn might be hurt by this, but she reported that the new wife appeared unfazed by it all and was just grateful there was hope for Levi's recovery. Besides, the old rancher seemed to be sparring with Aurelie in his delirium.

Rand scooted his microscope closer to the window and got the glass vials that contained the previous hair samples from a cabinet. "It's been a full day since I removed the bullet. Tabitha refused to leave his side last night, and I finally gave her a few blankets and she curled up on the floor. Her brothers seem quite indulgent of her."

"Josh says she and Levi always fuss with each other and speak their minds about things, but they have a special bond. If one of her brothers criticizes their father, she leaps like a tigress to his defense."

Rand adjusted the microscope, as he compared the specimens. "Well, I'll be."

"What?"

"We've got a match. Look." He stepped aside and let Danna look.

She was not certain what she was seeing. "They look the same to me."

"That's the point. They are, at least to the eye. What we don't know is how many other specimens might match. The science on such things is not far along."

"But you would bet these came from the same person?"

"Yes, if I were a betting man, that's how I'd place my bet."

"You would testify to that?"

"Yes. But if pressed, I would have to concede that the match cannot be confirmed with scientific certainty. Judge Robinson most definitely was not a match, however. Not even close."

"I'm just looking to establish reasonable doubt from Judge Robinson's standpoint. I'm going to report this to Marshal Calder. I'd like for him bring in Reverend Hiram Sibley before he pulls out of the territory."

47

TABITHA FOUND WOLF at his temporary down-town studio, bent over a work bench, apparently carving out a design of Navajo symbols on the top of a tea table he had fashioned. Ordinarily, she was unimpressed by the fine furniture owned by the wealthy, but she envied the person who had commissioned this piece.

He straightened and turned when she entered, and she slipped easily into his arms and lifted her head to accept his lingering kiss. She did not pull away. She had not seen him since he paused at the wagon bearing her wounded father on the journey to Santa Fe. She allowed herself to savor his closeness now.

"Would you be receiving guests at your lodge to-night?" she asked.

"Only one."

"I'll try to be there first."

"That should not be difficult. I'll prepare a fine dinner, if you desire."

"I desire. And I'll be in charge of everything else," she added suggestively.

"Then you will be an overnight guest?"

"Of course."

"Your mood tells me your father is improving."

"Yes. But I also saw my first League article in the *New Mexican* this morning. I am to write another for tomorrow's edition, and I will give that attention this afternoon. Thank you. Danna told me what you did. Among other things, you are an accomplished liar and blackmailer. Have you no limits to your talents?"

Wolf remained silent.

"Okay. Don't answer that. Anyway, I'm glad I'm back. Hopefully, I can keep you and Danna from going around killing people. But I'm really here this morning on a mission."

"A mission?"

"I want you to go with me to visit my father. I want him to meet the man who saved his life. He insists on seeing me alone this morning."

"If I'm with you, he won't be seeing you alone."

"He will understand. He's regained his sensibilities now, but he was saying very strange things when he was out of his head. Things about me and my mother. I can't explain it. I would just like you with me."

"Then I will go with you to see your father. When?"

"Now."

Fifteen minutes later, they entered Micah Rand's bare-bones clinic. Dr. Rand stuck his head into the waiting area and waived them through. "Your father kicked the rest of the family out of here," he said. "He's crabby, and he's taking charge. I take those as positive signs. Gertie's on an errand right now, but I told her not to let anyone else in. He's all yours. Let me know if he seems to be having problems."

When they entered the room, Levi was sitting up in his bed. He had been eating eggs and bread and other soft foods since the previous night, and Tabby no longer feared for his life. He appeared uncharacteristically nervous, though. Just like her. He looked at her and tendered a small smile and a nod.

He shot Wolf a suspicious glance, however. Tabitha moved quickly to his bedside and kissed his cheek. "Pop, I want you to meet Oliver Wolf. I've told you about him."

"Hello, Mr. Rivers. My pleasure," Wolf said. He moved nearer and offered his hand.

Levi weakly accepted Wolf's handshake. "Call me Levi. A man who saved my life shouldn't be calling me 'Mister.'"

"Pop, I didn't tell you everything about Oliver. I love him. And I trust him totally. I've asked him to be with me this morning. He can hear anything you want to say to me. Anything."

Levi studied Wolf's face, and their eyes locked. Then, he nodded his approval. "You two sit down," he said. "I'm going to tell you about Summer."

"Summer?"

"Yep. You look so damn much like her, it scares me sometimes. I should have told you about Summer a long time ago. Just never had the guts. Truth is I didn't want you to think less of me. But Aurelie came and said it's time. She was right about that."

"What are you talking about? Mom's been gone for almost seven years."

"Yeah. But she came to me up in the mountains when I thought I was going to die. Said it was time to tell you."

The business about her mother made Tabitha wonder if she should call Dr. Rand in, but she tossed the notion aside and decided she was getting tired of this dance. "Pop, I'm starting to get pissed. Say what you've got to say, or we're leaving." She looked at Wolf, whose dark eyes and impassive face warned her to be patient.

"Summer was the woman who gave birth to you," Levi said.

Her heart started racing and it felt like her body had numbed. Wolf's hand closed gently around hers, and a calm settled in.

"Just hear me out. Then do what you will." Levi began telling the story. Tears rolled down his cheeks when he told of his love affair with Summer and her unexpected death. His voice trembled and faltered as he spoke of taking Tabitha home to Aurelie, but it grew steadier as his story passed through the years, and he talked of the special place his daughter held in his heart. And then, he abruptly stopped talking and fastened his eyes on her face.

Tabitha was stunned speechless, fighting back tears. She wasn't the kind of woman who cried. Even during her darkest days with the Comanche, she had not shed a tear. It was only in the mountains, when she thought her father lay dead in front of her, that she had given in to tears. And now, she was nearly overwhelmed again. She started to get out of the chair and run, but Wolf held fast to her hand and would not allow her.

"Aurelie was right, Tabby. You needed to know about this. Summer is so much a part of what you are, you were entitled. I've been selfish. I just couldn't stand the thought of you seeing your old man's betrayal, but I've carried this guilt long enough. I've never been a man to make excuses. I did what I did. I broke my own code. If I'm going to be judged by the worst thing I've done in my life, then, if there's a God up there, he's going to show me the door to hell. And, you know, that's all right. Because one thing good came out of all of this, and she's sitting right here in this room. You're Summer's gift to the world. And I'm proud to be a part of it. I'll never say I'm sorry for that."

She did not know what to say. Wolf released her hand. She got up and moved closer to Levi's bedside and brushed her fingers down his stubbled cheek before she kissed him. "I love you, Pop. I have some work to do. And then, some thinking. You need a shave. If you want to chance me with a straight-edge, I'll come in and shave you tomorrow morning."

He smiled weakly. "I'd like that."

That evening, she and Wolf made frantic love, devoid of patience and tenderness. Afterward, cocooned in the robe and blankets covering the floor of their little lodge, she sobbed until she was all cried out, while Wolf silently held her naked body close.

Later, as she lay spooned against his back, Tabitha asked, "Pop's suffered, hasn't he? He's paid a price for that time nearly twenty-four years ago. He's punished himself more than any vengeful God could."

"You will sometimes find a man who lives by a code that doesn't leave much room for bending. When he breaks it, he carries the burden the rest of his days."

"You sound like a man who knows."

"Another story. Another time."

"I love you, Oliver Wolf. I don't give a damn what happened with you and your silly code."

48

MARSHAL CHANCE CALDER caught up with Wolf as he was opening his studio the next morning. Wolf had work to tend to. There was the commissioned tea tabletop he had hoped to finish today. And he had two hacienda renovations in progress that required some on-site supervision of his Mexican craftsmen. He prayed that the marshal would make his visit brief.

"Good morning, Oliver," the marshal said, "I need to speak with you a minute."

"A minute is about all I've got, Chance. I've got projects calling for my attention."

"I'd like to have you ride out to the Church of Miracles to back me up when I make an arrest."

"Sibley?"

"You and Miss Sinclair already eliminated the other two most likely prospects. Self-defense, so says you and the lady law wrangler. Sibley had a different story. Says you and she killed those unarmed men in cold blood."

"And you're asking for my help?"

"Well, those gunslingers didn't have any guns nearby when I got there, but it didn't seem to me they'd be wearing empty holsters for decorations. And I'd consider Miss Sinclair a reliable witness. Besides, she was the one who reported the shoot-out."

"I turned in my deputy's badge."

"You can pin it back on for an hour. Come on, Oliver. Help me out here. The sky's falling in since the newspaper started running your lady friend's stories. Have you read this morning's paper?"

"No." He had just left the naked reporter snuggled in her buffalo robe an hour earlier.

"Well, she's laying out names. The preacher. Simon Willard, the government's General Procurement Officer, and several ranchers and merchants. Claims she has evidence certain public officials have been covering up for the League. She says she'll write about that and old Levi's shooting tomorrow. The shit's flying, and I don't have enough shovels. And I don't know who to trust these days. Just help me out for a few days until things settle down. Tabitha Rivers is stirring a big pot. You can watch her back officially that way."

Wolf sighed. "All right. Two days and I'm a civilian again."

"For what it's worth, the Territorial Governor has requested that the Army put some troops at Fort Union on stand-by. The acting judge has been given information that Reginald Swayne may be involved in this League business some way. Danna Sinclair has even filed a motion with the court that he be disqualified as prosecutor in Judge Robinson's case because of possible conflict of interest."

"It sounds like Swayne's got his hands full."

"Yep. Supposedly, the U. S. Attorney General is sending a young special prosecutor by the name of Casey McGlaun out from Omaha, Nebraska to put things in order, along with a couple of deputy marshals to help me out. But that will take a couple of weeks."

"Then you're going to want my help for more than two days."

"Well, maybe part-time. You can look after your other business in between things."

Wolf extended his hand, palm upward. "Give me the badge. I guess Tabby started all this. The least I can do is help you clean it up."

49

"YOU DIDN'T TELL me we were arresting Sibley for Constanza Robinson's murder," Wolf said after they locked the cell door on the self-ordained preacher. "I thought it was for his involvement with the League."

"Well, to my notion, the criminal charges are kind of shaky. All they got is a hair from his privates that might be a match to one found on Mrs. Robinson. I was worried he might be out of the territory before charges get filed for the League business, so this gives me an excuse to hold him a spell."

"So, you're holding two men for the same crime?"

"I am. By rights, Judge Robinson should be released, but the prosecutor is under a cloud. I think Marty Locke's going to file a motion with the acting judge tomorrow to grant bond to Judge Robinson, given the legal mess we got in Santa Fe. At least he would get out of here."

"Would you care if I had a chat with Preacher Sibley?"

"You can't hurt him, you know? At least not in a way that leaves any marks."

"I won't hurt him. Could you bring the judge up here a spell, so he won't hear what we're saying?"

"Sure, I can do that. I'll fix him a cup of coffee. He's not so bad to talk to, now that he's been tossed from his high horse."

Wolf went back to Sibley's cell while Chase Calder moved Judge Robinson up to his office. Sibley was sitting on the straw-mattress cot in the cell, and Wolf sat down on the wood bench that was the nearest thing to a chair the box-like room offered. He remained silent and sat there for several minutes, studying Hiram Sibley's face, wondering if he was, in fact, Constanza Robinson's killer.

"What are you looking at, Breed?" Sibley glared back at Wolf, his ice-blue eyes showing his contempt.

"Just wondering if you are willing to hang for something you didn't do."

"You don't think I killed Constanza Robinson?"

"Doesn't make sense somehow. But the marshal's got some proof that might put a rope around your neck."

"I was there that night, but I didn't kill her."

"Care to talk about it? The League's falling apart. The stories in the *New Mexican* are laying out the prosecutor's case. Somebody in the chain is going to break it wide open to save their own hide. But you're not going to get the noose for fraud and bribery. And it might go easier for you to cooperate. Something to think about."

"I'll think about it. But I didn't kill Connie. I was in love with her. I went to the house that night. She was the same as usual, except she was in a rush to get to bed and get it done. No complaint there. Afterward, I told her I wanted her to go away with me. I've been turning my properties into cash as fast as I can, and I wanted to disappear with her. And then she told me she was carrying our baby, and that made me all the crazier. She said she wouldn't leave her father and family in Santa Fe. Then she told me she would stay with the judge. He wouldn't divorce her or kick her out because of the scandal it would cause. As far as anybody else knew, the child would be theirs."

"She was telling you it was over for the two of you?"

"I took it that way, but she left a possibility. She said if the judge would happen to die, that would change things. We could get together after some time passed and stay in Santa Fe."

"I gather she was suggesting you help the judge die?"

"I took it that way. She was in a hurry for me to leave that night. Said she was going to her father's hacienda for a few days and had to get ready. That fit perfectly with my plans for firing the house. I didn't want to kill anybody, least of all her . . . just then."

"What do you mean?"

"When I headed back to the church, I was thinking of ways I might get rid of Judge Andrew Robinson. Less than two days later, I found out somebody else had been screwing the Mexican whore. I went from grief to hate fast as the crack of a whip. If she hadn't been already dead, I might have been up to the killing then."

"How did you find that out?" Wolf asked.

"Now I'm getting into League business. I guess I've got nothing to lose. It happened this way. Reggie Swayne came out to the church after that reporter bitch came to his office. He said she was after the League like a hound after a fox, and I'd better shut her up quick. That's how I came to send a few of the boys for a visit."

Wolf had known of Sibley's involvement in Tabitha's beating, but somehow the confirmation of it ignited his fury, and it was all he could do to restrain himself from snapping the man's neck. He took a deep breath and continued. "But Swayne said something about Mrs. Robinson, also?"

"Yeah, she had been screwing him regular, too. And he was in love with her and had plans of his own. He was falling apart over fear that his affair with Connie would come out. He was about to piss his britches at the idea it would all blow up in his face. He could become a suspect, and, at the least, have an embarrassing conflict of interest. He said that the judge was bound to turn on the League and that we couldn't chance him getting to trial. I took that to mean the judge needed to die. The second time in about as many days the judge's death had been recommended to me."

"Obviously, you didn't take the bait."

"Well, I did. I was just thinking out how to make it happen without suspicion coming my way."

"Do you think Swayne killed Mrs. Robinson?"

"No, I don't. He was hurting too much. I didn't say anything about my involvement with her. I wanted to stay off any suspect list, and I'd decided somebody gave her what she had coming. I was relieved that maybe it wasn't my child that died with her. Could have belonged to any male in Santa Fe, except her husband, it appears."

"Who do you think killed her, just for the sake of speculation?"

Sibley responded instantly. "Her husband."

"You sound quite positive."

"I can't think of anybody who had a better reason."

Wolf got up from the bench. "Not yet, anyway. Can I tell Marshal Calder that you will talk to him about the League?"

"Yeah. I'll tell him everything he wants to know and probably quite a lot more. I figure the law really wants to nail Simon Willard, and I'm the best witness to that. My stories might change, though, if I don't strike a deal that suits me."

50

TABITHA SAT AT a table for two in the Exchange dining room, waiting for Wolf to join her for a prearranged lunch. She was mildly annoyed by his tardiness. Her aggravation dissipated instantly when she caught sight of him entering the room, his buckskin shirt stretched against his muscular arms and sheathed torso. He walked slowly toward her, and she noted that the eyes of every woman in the dining room followed him. She wondered if he knew he had that effect on women. Probably. Damn him. But she reminded herself she was the only one who shared his blankets. That thought aroused her, and she thought of suggesting they skip lunch.

"Sorry I'm late, I've been working on your story."

Tabitha's reporting passion kicked her libido aside. "You've got something new on the League?"

"I'm starving. Let's order first."

"You're torturing me."

"My stomach's suffering."

They ordered shredded beef sandwiches and apple pie with coffee. While they waited for the order, Tabitha decided to press Wolf for his information. "Tell me what you've learned. Please."

"First, we must have an understanding." He pointed to the deputy marshal's badge pinned on his shirt. "I am now a temporary deputy again. Most of what I've learned has been in that capacity. I will tell you some things that are not for publication, if you promise not to write about it. I will decide what you can write about and what you cannot. Can you agree to that?"

"I'm not so sure about that. What if I do not?"

"Then I tell you absolutely nothing."

"I thought I was in love with you. But you're showing a mean streak."

"You still love me. You just don't like it when you don't get your way. Levi spoiled you rotten. I won't. Sometimes."

"All right. Tell me. You can be my censor, and what I do write will be attributed to a reliable source."

Their meals arrived, and, while they ate, Wolf related his conversation with Hiram Sibley. "I don't think Mrs. Robinson's lovers should be mentioned by name.

Her pregnancy was already reported in an earlier story. I would have no problem with your writing that a reliable source disclosed that the marshal's office is investigating an allegation that a public official was engaged in a relationship with the deceased. I cleared that with Chance. That would get Swayne's attention and probably shake things up some."

"I still don't like the idea of being told what I can publish, but I don't think it serves any purpose to muddy Constanza's name any more than necessary to lead us to the truth. I assume I can say it has been confirmed that a high-level League member has admitted to ordering the fire and my beating."

"Yes. And I think, soon enough, we'll be able to authorize release of the name."

"I can live with this. For now."

"Good. Now, tell me about your father. Did you visit him this morning?"

"Yes. Dr. Rand thinks he can be turned loose in a few days. He may need a cane to steady him until the dizziness goes away. I got there early before any of the brothers showed up, and we talked about Summer. He really loved her, Oliver. It may have been wrong, but it wasn't a sordid, casual thing. And what can I say? If Summer had not come into his life, I would not be sitting here talking to you."

"That would be a tragedy for me."

"What's done is done. Everything we experience makes us what we are. I can rewrite a story before it hits the press. I can even retract something I've already had published. But we cannot rewrite the stories of our lives. We can only move on to the next chapter and try to make it the best one yet." She looked at him and wondered if he thought she was crazy, rambling philosophical like this.

Wolf returned a closed-lips smile. "You should write that down in your journal. I'll try to remember those wise words myself."

"Anyway, I love Pop, and I'll always love and remember Mom for taking me in. But I do want to find Summer's family. I want to know more about her and that part of my heritage. Pop gave me some clues and said I should go searching in Taos. I told him about the Navajo woman who approached me the morning after the fire. He wondered if it could have been Summer's sister."

"It sounds to me like you've got another quest. And another story."

He was on to her. She was going to have few secrets with this man. "I have a story for tomorrow's issue to write. I've got to run. I'll see you at home tonight."

"Home? You mean at the lodge?"

"Home is where you are, my love."

51

TABITHA HAD OPENED the door of the *New Mexican* when the thought struck her. She backed out onto the boardwalk and shut the door behind her. She needed to interview Carly, Judge Robinson's favorite prostitute. Jael had shared only a sketch of the woman's relationship with the judge, given that the lawyers did not want any testimony or evidence leaking to the press. Tabitha had also met her briefly this morning when she stopped at the house she and Danna owned to change into a dress and what she called her town clothes. Carly was temporarily hiding out there, but Tabitha thought the public disclosure of the League's activities should have substantially reduced any danger the woman might be in. She had not had an opportunity to talk to her at the house because Danna was present, and Carly was putting on what Jael had earlier told her, was the woman's "I don't speak English" act.

It occurred to Tabitha, from Jael's remarks, that Carly Reyes might be the only witness not involved in the League organization who could identify the major participants, including Eve Cambridge and Simon Willard. She was not off limits for an interview, and she might have the knowledge to help Tabitha tie everything together in a neat package. As a bonus, she would be a key witness if Judge Andrew Robinson should be tried for the murder of his wife. She had to talk to this woman before she wrote another word. She walked briskly to the Exchange stable to retrieve Smokey. She did not ride sidesaddle, so she knew there would be a few shocked whispers on the street when they rode out. She didn't give a damn. When the new house was completed, she vowed she would work from home and send all her work out by messenger and never squirm into a dress again. On second thought, she conceded she would have to keep a few skirts for special occasions.

When she arrived at the house, she entered without knocking—it was her house after all—and found Carly sitting in the rocking chair, attired in bloomers and a camisole and smoking a cigarette. At least she was holding a tea cup for her ashes. Tabitha noted that the woman also had what appeared to be a skinny sheath at her hip, suspended from a rawhide strip that wrapped around her waist. Strange. Carly looked up, seemingly unsurprised at the visit. Tabitha took a seat on the settee and plucked her notepad and pencil from her big pocketbook.

"We spoke briefly this morning," Tabitha said. "But you appeared not to understand me. I didn't say anything then, but I happen to know you speak perfect English, so we can brush the language game aside from the beginning."

The young woman was quite beautiful, but her looks were not enhanced by the scowl on her face. "I know who you are," Carly said. "I don't have anything to say for your newspaper."

"What if I pay you for an interview?"

Carly's eyes brightened with interest. "How much?"

"How much do you make in a week when you are working?"

"At least twenty-five dollars for my share."

Tabitha figured the woman was lying, but said, "I'll pay you fifty dollars for an interview. I can write you a draft on the Second National Bank right now. You can cash it on your way out of town. You are leaving, aren't you?"

"How did you know?"

"The packed carpet bag near the door is a hint of your plans."

"Okay. Give me the money. I'll be gone before anything I say hits the newspaper."

Tabitha found a blank bank draft in her pocketbook and confirmed her Derringer pocket was unfastened while she was searching. "What name do I put on the draft?"

"Carmencita Reyes." She spelled her first name.

Tabitha reached out and handed her the draft, which Carly folded and tucked into her bosom. "When we are finished," Tabitha said, "I intend to inform Danna Sinclair and the marshal's office you are planning to leave town. You are a potential witness in multiple criminal cases."

Anger flashed in the young woman's eyes. "They can't force me to stay. Andrew said I am required to be served with a subpoena first and then I can be arrested only if I fail to appear to testify. They must find me first. Get to your interview."

"Very well. You mentioned Andrew. I assume you are referring to Judge Andrew Robinson?"

"Of course."

"Was he training you to be a lawyer when he explained a witness's rights?"

"What kind of question is that? No, we just talked about things like that sometimes, and I remembered what he told me."

"This is not for publication. But did you and the Judge talk a lot? Were you more than his prostitute?"

"He loved me."

"I find this interesting, since I was informed he thought you did not speak English. I don't understand why he would explain the law to you, if he thought you were not capable of understanding. You lied to Jael and Danna about that, but you forgot to lie to me. Or are you lying to me now? I'm very confused."

"I thought this interview was about the League."

"But you were the judge's link to the League. The communication went from Willard to Eve, and then from her to you and to the judge and back."

"Who told you that? Sibley? He's talking, isn't he?"

"It just makes sense. The judge has refused to talk. His lawyers thought he was trying to protect himself from recriminations by the League. I think he was more concerned about protecting you. The world is full of men doing stupid things for the love of a woman. I think he fell in love with you. His wife didn't understand him or appreciate him. You made it your business to do just that. I'm sure it was simple for you."

"As a matter of fact, it was."

"Did you expect him to leave his wife? Then, after a respectable time, you would be the wife of the Territorial Judge?"

"He would have left her, if she had not told him that night about the expected baby. Then he had to kill her."

"He didn't kill her. You did. He's protecting you."

Carly Reyes's mouth tightened and her fists clenched, and Tabitha could see that her composure was cracking. She glared at Tabitha with seething contempt.

"He told you, didn't he? The whiney son of a bitch told you. I knew he'd cave. That's why I'm getting out of this town."

Tabitha played along. "He didn't tell me how it happened."

"He left the hotel and was supposed to demand a divorce. He had the grounds. Adultery. But then she told him about the baby, and he lost his nerve. He told me he considered killing her, but he couldn't. I put him to sleep. He was like a drugged man after sex. And then I went to the hacienda and did the job that should have been his. I didn't tell him what I had done, but he knew. And he still wanted me. Besides, I was his alibi."

Tabitha had no idea Constanza Robinson's murder was going to be the story when she purchased her interview with Carly Reyes. It had just fallen into place, word by word. Now what? She was dealing with a dangerous woman. She inched her fingers into her handbag to remove the Derringer waiting there. But she was not fast enough. Carly sprang on her like a mountain cat, and they flew off the settee together as it tumbled over.

Carly landed on top of Tabitha, who rolled just as the young woman's arm swung down with the stiletto. The narrow blade easily sliced through Tabitha's dress and drove into the fleshy cheek of her buttocks. Her panic overrode the pain, and her eyes were searching vainly for a weapon, when she saw the bloody knife blade arcing toward her throat. Still pinned by Carly on the floor, she thrust her head away, and the stiletto missed by an inch. As Carly pulled back to strike again, Tabitha locked both hands on Carly's forearm and twisted, hoping to dislodge the weapon. The small woman had the edge with gravity on her side, coupled with surprising strength, and the knife inched toward Tabitha's neck. She could feel her arms weakening and beginning to cave, and then, with all the strength she could muster, she yanked Carly's arm sideways. In the same instant, Tabitha raised her head and latched onto the knife hand with her teeth, the spike-like stiletto blade just inches from her cheek. She sunk her teeth deeply into the hand and held on fast, tearing into bone and tendon while Carly screamed and finally released her grip on the knife, dropping it on the floor.

Tabitha seized the moment and flipped Carly off, and, in the same motion, snatched up the stiletto. She got up on her knees and spat the blood and pieces of flesh from her mouth. Carly moaned and shrieked as she rolled on the floor, clutching her mangled hand. Tabitha retrieved her Derringer before she assessed her situation. It was only then that she saw her own blood-drenched skirt and began to tear it off. Her wound was stinging, but as much as she could determine without a mirror, the bleeding had slowed to a trickle. It was more a puncture than a slash. She found several tea towels to stuff down her underpants to staunch the bleeding.

She then turned her attention to Carly, keeping her Derringer within easy reach. The young prostitute was focused on her shredded hand, however, and was silent and compliant while Tabitha bound the hand with another towel and strips of cloth.

There was no time to dress for the occasion, so a short while later, two half-clothed, bloodied women, Carly astride Smokey, appeared at the Plaza on their way to Dr. Micah Rand's office. As the crowd gathered to watch the spectacle, Tabitha hollered for someone to fetch Marshal Calder.

52

"HOW IS YOUR butt holding up?" Wolf asked.

"My butt's just fine, thank you, as if you didn't know," Tabitha replied.

"Two days in the saddle can make a sore spot sorer."

"I'm fine." Her butt hurt like blazes, but she wasn't going to admit it to him.

It had been ten days, and she thought that was plenty of healing time. Wolf had warned her they should wait, but she wanted to get the trip done before winter. It was important.

Wolf mounted on Owl and Tabitha riding Smokey, they rode side-by-side at a walk, so they could converse easily. The snow had not moved down from the high country yet, and a radiant sun in a clear azure sky relegated heavy coats to the pack horse. It was a good day to be alive. Then, again, she decided, every day was a good day to be alive.

"I didn't mention it before," Wolf said, "Josh said we could stay with them in their house this winter, while ours is being built."

"That would put one of the kids out of a bedroom."

"Well, I guess you could stay with Danna when the weather turns bad. You still own half the house."

"I don't think so. I don't think it's long before Dr. Rand is making house calls there. I'd be in the way."

"What? Oh, I see."

"Why don't we share Josh's and Jael's house days, and sleep in our lodge nights? We'd have our privacy when it counted."

"Well, I guess that would be fine by me."

"Jael and I have already agreed to it."

"I should have known."

"Days, I'm going to work at one house or the other. I'm not going in to the *New Mexican* much anymore. I'll send some stories over, but I've got to have the manuscript for *Dismal Trail* to the publisher by spring. The publisher says non-fiction stuff doesn't make a lot of money, but it might be around for some years. *Last Hunt* is turning into a gold mine. I might try another novel."

"Sounds like a quiet time ahead."

"I would like to learn more about what's happening up in Wyoming and Montana with the Sioux and Cheyenne. That seems to be where the Army action is going to be during the next few years."

"First, you have the League trials to cover. And Carly Reyes's murder trial."

"Simon Willard and Eve Cambridge have disappeared. Until they're found, the League stories don't offer a lot of excitement. The murder trial will catch a lot headlines, though. Carly would be the first woman hanged in New Mexico Territory. I don't get any pleasure out of being a part of that history."

"The judge will see some jail time over his part in the League, and, possibly, as an accessory to the murder. He may share a cell with Reginald Swayne."

"Danna thinks the judge and Reggie will get off with disbarment, especially if they don't bring Willard in to testify. She said the judge's big risk is that Carly would make a deal to testify about the judge's League involvement in exchange for a lesser murder charge that would let her escape the noose."

"Changing the subject," Wolf said, "look north. You can see the pueblos."

A chill danced down Tabitha's spine. She found herself suddenly a bit frightened. "I hope this is the right thing to do."

"If it's not, I suspect you will still find a story there."

He always knew how to reach her. She kneed Smokey into a faster gait, and Wolf followed. Soon they arrived in the sleepy, dusty town of Taos. Tabitha could not believe it when she saw the attractive Navajo woman on the side of the street—the same woman she had encountered weeks earlier in Santa Fe. Tabitha reined in and dismounted and walked up to the woman, whose warm eyes and smile welcomed her.

"I am Summer's child," Tabitha said.

"I know. I have been waiting for you."

Made in United States
Troutdale, OR
07/20/2023

11448024R00213